BOOKS BY ALAN PATON

Cry, The Beloved Country
Too Late The Phalarope
South Africa In Transition
Tales From A Troubled Land

*Too Late
the Phalarope*

TOO LATE
THE PHALAROPE

by

ALAN

PATON

Charles Scribner's Sons

NEW YORK

Too Late
the Phalarope

I

Perhaps I could have saved him, with only a word, two words, out of my mouth. Perhaps I could have saved us all. But I never spoke them.

Strange it is that one could run crying to the house of a man that one loved, to save him from danger, and that he could say to one, *have I not told you not to come to this house?* And strange it is that one should withdraw silent and shamed.

For he spoke hard and bitter words to me, and shut the door of his soul on me, and I withdrew. But I should have hammered on it, I should have broken it down with my naked hands, I should have cried out there not ceasing, for behind it was a man in danger, the bravest and gentlest of them all. So I who came to save was made a supplicant; and because of the power he had over me, *I held,* in the strange words of the English, *I held my peace.*

Yet I should have cried out my knowledge at him, it might have saved him, it might have saved us all. Then may the Lord Jesus Christ have mercy upon me, that I held the peace that was no peace at all.

1

And why did I not speak? For I was old and he was young, he was always a boy to me; but it was he that had the power.

I knew him from the day he was born, for I was his father's sister, and lived with them all in the house; and he and his father both had the power over me. His father was a giant of a man, and the boy grew as tall and broad as he; but the boy Pieter had something of the woman in him, and the father none at all until it was too late.

The boy was gentle and eager to please, tender to women and children, even the black children on the farm. He was always reading books, but his father read only the One, and the newspapers. There were strange things in the boy's mind that none of us knew or understood.

I remember once he was reading some English book in the house, and outside our neighbours' boys were shooting at three tins on a stump. His father was restless, and at last he said to the boy, is that the way to treat your friends? Or are you afraid to shoot? The boy got up and went out, and my brother got up too, stiffly because of his leg, and went to the window to watch. Then the boy took the gun from one of the neighbours' boys, and fired three times at the tins, and shot them all down from the stump. Then he called all his friends, and they went off to some other place and pleasure. My brother came back from the window with the heavy face that forbade one to speak to him; one could not know if he were proud or pleased or angry. For the truth was he had fathered a strange son, who had all his father's will and strength, and could outride and outshoot them all, yet had all the gentleness of a girl, and strange unusual thoughts in his mind, and a passion for books and learning, and a passion for the flowers of veld and kloof, so that he would bring them into the house and hold them in his hands, as though there were some deep meaning that he was finding in them. Had he been one or the other, I think his father would have understood him better, but he was both. And when you despised the one, the other would shoot three tins from the stump; and when you approved the one, the other would sit like a girl with a flower.

He was always two men. The one was the soldier of the war, with all the English ribbons that his father hated; the lieutenant in the police, second only to the captain; the great rugby player, hero of thousands of boys and men. The other was the dark and silent man, hiding from all men his secret knowledge of himself, with that hardness and coldness that made men afraid of him, afraid even to speak to him. Yet I should have spoken, God forgive me that I did not speak, when I should have cried out not ceasing. For the secret knowledge came to me, and could have been used for his salvation, before it came to that other who used it for his destruction.

And I write it all down here, the story of our destruction. And if I write it with fear, then it is not so great a fear, I being myself destroyed. And if I write it down, maybe it will cease to trouble my mind. And if I write it down, people may know that he was two men, and that one was brave and gentle; and they may know, when they judge and condemn, that this one struggled with himself in darkness and alone, calling on his God and on the Lord Jesus Christ to have mercy on him. Therefore when the other Pieter van Vlaanderen did not entreat, this one entreated; and when the other did not repent, this one repented; and because the other did not entreat nor repent, he was destroyed, and because there is no such magic, this one, the brave and gentle, was destroyed with him.

I did not observe all these events. Yet because I am apart, being disfigured, and not like other women, yet because in my heart I am like any other woman, and because I am apart, so living apart and watching I have learned to know the meaning of unnoticed things, of a pulse that beats suddenly, and a glance that moves from here to there because it wishes to rest on some quite other place. And later, much was shown to me, not only by others, but in the things, lonely and terrible, that he wrote in his secret book, and when he was in prison. And God forgive me that I do not always understand His ways. Small strength, small weakness, that I understand; but why a man should have great strength and great weakness I do not understand. For the first calls him to honour, and the second to dishonour; and the first to fame, and the second to destruction. Yet it comes to me that it is not the judgment of God but that of men which is a stranger to compassion; for the Lord said, go thou and sin no more. And this may anger some, but I am beyond anger and loss, being, as the world sees it, myself destroyed.

Ah, he was like his mother, tender and gentle. For though I loved her son, perhaps beyond all wisdom, yet she never denied me, nor did it ever cause a word between us, not even the word that is buried deep and never spoken. If ever a woman was all love, it was she, all love and care. Her smile was the smile of love and care, tender yet always anxious, most of all when she smiled at her son. The black moods and the coldness, the gentleness and the tenderness,

the shooting and the riding and the books, the strange
authority, she pondered them all in her heart, waiting the
day that never came, when the hidden turbulence would die
down, and the boy be whole and at peace. And my brother,
if he pondered them, did so with the anger of a man cheated
with a son, who was like a demon with a horse, and like a
pale girl with a flower.

All these things I will write down, yet it is not only that
they trouble my mind; nor is it only that I may show that
though one neither entreated nor repented, the other did
both entreat and repent; nor is it only that men may have
more knowledge of compassion. For I also remember the
voice that came to John in Patmos, saying, what thou seest,
write it in a book, and though I do not dare to claim a knowledge of this voice, yet do I dare to claim a knowledge of
some voice. Therefore I put aside my fears, and am obedient.

II

The lieutenant was in Pretorius Street, in the shadow of the tall gum trees, when he heard the sound of bare feet running. Pretorius Street is the street that goes to the black people's location; there are no lights there because there are no lights in any streets in Venterspan. The only lights at all, except those in the houses, are in van Onselen Street, the tarred road that goes north through the grass country to Johannesburg, and south to Natal and Zululand, and these lights came from Abraham Kaplan's hotel, The Royal, and Matthew Kaplan's store, The Southern Transvaal Trading Company, and Labuschagne's Service Station.

When he heard the sound of the running he drew back into the shadow of the gums and the girl ran past him, so close that he could have touched her. Her breath came with a kind of moaning, but she was hardly past him when she stopped running, though he could still hear the sound of her breathing. Then he heard her moving also into the shadows of the trees, and brushing against the weeds of the vacant ground. Then he knew she had lain down, and was trying to control her gasping.

He waited till her pursuer was abreast of him, then he suddenly moved out and caught him by the arm. The man tried to escape from him, but he let him struggle in silence. Neither spoke a word, they stood there locked, one calm, powerful, hardly moving, the other in terror. Then the captive stopped struggling, and stood with his chin on his breast, not resting on it, but thrust into it with all the force of fear and desperation. The lieutenant put his free hand round the man's jaws, and as quietly as he had stopped and held him, he got his fingers under the chin. He forced the head up slowly, and knew by the feel of the skin that the man was only a boy.

The boy's eyes were tight closed, and the face was tight too, as though he would shut out any likeness of himself, or any fear. But the lieutenant knew that he was in fear, and took away his hand.

— Who are you, he asked in Afrikaans.

But the boy dropped his head again, and made no answer. The lieutenant lifted the head once more, so that it was turned up to his own, but the eyes would not open. Then he knew who it was.

— Who are you, he asked in English.

The boy's face loosened, and there was a frightened and urgent appeal in it.

— Dick.

— Yes.

— Open your eyes.

The boy opened his eyes.

— Dick, do you know me?

— No.

— Take your time.

The boy looked at him again, and the lieutenant took
away his hand. Then the terror came back to the boy's face,
and he dropped his head.

— Do you know me?

— Yes, lieutenant.

— What were you doing?

The boy made no answer, so the lieutenant spoke to him
in a tone of authority.

— Answer me.

— I was walking along van Onselen Street . . .

Then he would not go on.

— Yes.

— I saw someone running . . .

— Yes.

— He looked as though he had done something.

— Done something?

— Yes.

— What?

— You know, stolen or something.

— So you chased him?

— Yes.

The lieutenant released his hold on the boy's arm, and
leant back against the tree. He took out his pipe and matches,
and the boy looked round with apprehension.

— You'd rather I didn't smoke, Dick?

But the boy did not answer. The lieutenant stood away
from the tree.

— Come with me, Dick.

— Where to, lieutenant?

— To my house.

But the boy did not move.

— All right, go on by yourself. Tell Mrs. van Vlaanderen I told you to come. Tell her I wanted to talk to you about rugby football.

He looked at his watch.

— Say I told you to come at eight-thirty.

— Yes, lieutenant.

When the boy had gone, the lieutenant walked on a few paces, and called out quietly to the girl.

— You can come out now, he said.

So the girl came out and stood before him submissively.

— Who are you?

— Stephanie, *baas*.

And the lieutenant said, I did not recognize you, Stephanie.

For Stephanie was well-known to the police and the courts. She was twenty-three, or twenty-five perhaps, and her father and her mother were unknown, and there was a good deal of lightness in her colour. But she lived in the black people's location with the old woman Esther, who was said to be more than a hundred years old. Some said that Esther was a child when our white people first came trekking into the grass country, and it was true that she herself told of it, but I think it was only an old woman's vanity. Stephanie looked after her, and kept her alive by brewing and selling liquor, which is against the law, and brought her often into the courts. She was a strange creature, this girl Stephanie, with a secret embarrassed smile that was the mark of her strangeness. She took her sentences smiling and frowning, and would go smiling and frowning out of the court to the prison, and would come out from the prison smiling and frowning, and make more liquor, and go back smiling and frowning to the court. She had a child whose father was unknown, and she kept it at some place in the reserve, in Maduna's country. And she had a queer look of innocence also, though she was no stranger to those things which are supposed to put an end to innocence.

— Why did you run, Stephanie?

— I do not want trouble, she said.

— What did he do?

— *Baas*, he asked me my name.

And you must know that in our country one does not go into a darkened street, and ask a black girl for her name.

— Who was it, Stephanie?

— I know, she said.

— You know?

— I know well, she said.

— What will you do?

— What should I do, she said.

— You know who I am?

— *Baas*, I know well.

The lieutenant stood there and considered it.

— This would bring great trouble for the man, he said.

— Yes, *baas*.

— You know his mother?

— I know her well.

— It would kill her.

She made a noise of assent and sympathy, but he knew he was talking of things outside her world, for she had been often enough to prison, and no one had died of it.

— I can believe it, she said obediently.

— Go home, then, Stephanie.

— Good night, *baas*.

So there she went, with knowledge to destroy a man. He thought he had perhaps been foolish. Perhaps he should have ordered her to keep her mouth shut, or he would make trouble for her. But the truth is that it was not in him to do such a thing.

He walked briskly back to van Onselen Street with its three rings of light in the mist. There was no one in the streets, and it struck the half-hour from the dark tower of the great Church, which stands like a watchman over the town and the grass country. He turned into one of the short earth roads that run off van Onselen Street, dark with trees, not gums but pines, giving back the sound of the wind. And then he was at the gate of his own house, one of our old-fashioned houses, with a narrow closed-in stoep, and col-oured diamond panes at each end of it, set into the wall.

III

His wife Nella was talking to the boy Dick when he went into the house. He kissed her, and said to Dick, sorry to keep you waiting. But the boy did not answer, he only smiled at the lieutenant out of a pale strained face.

— Come to my study, Dick. It's the only place I get any peace. Nella, are you going to make coffee for us?

— Of course, she said.

When they were in the study, he closed the door and made the boy sit down, and offered him a cigarette.

— We can smoke now, he said.

When his pipe was alight and the boy was smoking, but not easily, with constraint, he said, you've lots of friends, boys and girls. Your mother doesn't keep you tied up, does she?

— No, lieutenant.

— Then why do you do it, Dick?

At last the boy said, do what, lieutenant?

— What you were doing?

— It looked suspicious, lieutenant. I thought he might have stolen something.

— It wasn't a man, said the lieutenant, it was a girl.

— I thought it was a man.

— It was a girl, said the lieutenant, and if I go down to the location, I can find her in half an hour. I can find out what frightened her.

There was a knock on the door, and Nella came in with the coffee, and some rusks to eat with it.

— You'll eat the best rusks in the Transvaal tonight, said the lieutenant.

— Pieter, I'm going to bed.

He rose and kissed her.

— I shan't be long, he said.

When she had gone, and the door was shut again, and they had eaten the rusks and drunk the coffee in silence, he addressed the boy gravely.

— You know the Immorality Act?

— Yes, lieutenant.

— The police have had instructions to enforce the Immorality Act without fear or favour. Whether you're old or young, rich or poor, respected or nobody, whether you're a Cabinet Minister or a *predikant* or a headmaster or a tramp, if you touch a black woman and you're discovered, nothing'll save you.

— Yes, lieutenant.

— Then why did you do it?

— I know all that, lieutenant. But I didn't do it.

— Listen to me, Dick. No, don't look at me, look where you were looking before. I'm not talking to you as a policeman. I'm talking as your friend, your football captain. Do you understand me?

— Yes.

— Then why did you do it?

The boy struggled with himself. Then the note of authority returned to the lieutenant's voice.

— Dick, answer me.

— Lieutenant, I can't give any other answer. I tell you I *didn't* do it.

The lieutenant stood up.

— All right, Dick. You can go home.

He put on his overcoat, and the boy watched him miserably.

— What are you going to do, lieutenant?

— I'm going to the location.

The boy stood up too.

— Don't you see, it will look . . .

— It won't look anything. If I'm wrong, no one will hear a word.

He went and stood by the switch.

— You can go home, he said.

— Just let me explain something, lieutenant.

So the lieutenant sat down again.

— Lieutenant, I knew it was a girl. But I honestly thought she'd stolen something. You see, she . . .

— Yes, I know, she was running. Then can't you see that I'll still have to find her?

He stood up again.

— I'll tell you the truth, lieutenant.

— All right, Dick.

The boy stood in front of him, with his tongue playing on his dry lips.

The lieutenant said to him, sit down. And talk without fear, you understand?

The boy sat down, and at last he said, I frightened her.

— How?

— I spoke to her.

— What did you say?

— I asked her her name.

— Go on.

— That was all, lieutenant.

— Why did you ask her name?

But the boy had no answer for such a question.

— You mean, if she had been willing, you'd have gone with her.

— Yes, lieutenant.

— How often have you done it before? Look down there, and shut your eyes, and give the honest answer to yourself. Then give it to me.

The boy was silent a long time before he spoke.

— Three times, he said.

— How far did it go?

— Not further than that.

—٠ Just asking the name?

— Yes.

— Were you frightened?

— Yes.

The lieutenant was silent for a while, then he said gently, and why, Dick?

— I don't know.

— You know it would finish you for life. And kill your mother perhaps. And do God knows what to your sister.

— I know. I'll never do it again, lieutenant.

— When the police see a white man hanging about the streets, in any village or city, however harmless he thinks he looks, they watch him, often when he doesn't know. So never hang round the streets, and if you go out somewhere at night, go quickly, do you hear?

— Yes, lieutenant.

— It's a thing that's never forgiven, never forgotten. The court may give you a year, two years. But outside it's a sentence for life. Do you know that?

— Yes.

— You can go home, Dick.

At the gate the boy listened, up and down the road.

— Lieutenant.

— Yes.

— I don't know what to say to you, lieutenant.

— Yes.

— I'm glad you caught me, the boy whispered. I'm glad it was you, I mean.

Then when the lieutenant made no answer, he said, still in the whisper, I mean both things, I mean I'm glad I was caught, and glad it was you that caught me.

— I'm glad too, said the lieutenant. Tell your mother you were with me. Rugby. Goodnight, Dick.

He stood at the gate and watched the boy disappear into the darkness, walking lightly and swiftly, towards van Onselen Street.

The whole town was dark and silent, except for the barking of some dog, and the sound of ten o'clock striking from the tower of the church. The mist had gone and the stars shone down on the grass country, on the farms of his nation and people, Buitenverwagting and Nooitgedacht, Weltevreden and Dankbaarheid, on the whole countryside that they had bought with years of blood and sacrifice; for they had trekked from the British Government with its officials and its missionaries and its laws that made a black man as good as his master, and had trekked into a continent, dangerous and trackless, where wild beasts and savage men, and grim and waterless plains, had given way before their fierce will to be separate and survive. Then out of the harsh world of rock and stone they had come to the grass country, all green and smiling, and had given to it the names of peace and thankfulness. They had built their houses and their churches; and as God had chosen them for a people, so did they choose him for their God, cherishing their separateness that was now His Will. They set their conquered enemies apart, ruling them with unsmiling justice, declaring "no equality in Church or State", and making the iron law that no white man might touch a black woman, nor might any white woman be touched by a black man.

And to go against this law, of a people of rock and stone in a land of rock and stone, was to be broken and destroyed.

He turned slowly and walked into the house, and shut the door behind him. He put out the lights, and went quietly into the bedroom.

Nella had left the small light burning, and he stood and looked down at his children, at the six-year-old boy and the three-year-old girl. The boy slept with his fist against his cheek, after the manner of some wise man. The man was filled with tender feeling, and thrust his giant finger into the shut hand, and the small fingers closed over it, with trust and physical warmth. He bent down, himself forgotten, his face lit up with love and pride. He removed his finger, and kissed the boy and the girl. Then he undressed quietly, and having put out the small light, knelt at his bed. He was tired and said very little, except to make his petition, as he had done almost every night of his life, for his wife and his children, his father and mother and brothers and sisters, his aunt that lived single in his father's house, his wife's father and mother and brothers and sisters. Then he thought of the boy Dick, and prayed, *O God wees hom genadig, Here Jesus wees hom genadig*, which is God have mercy upon him, Lord Jesus have mercy upon him; then he was whispering, *O God wees my genadig, Here Jesus wees my genadig*, which is, God have mercy upon me, Lord Jesus have mercy upon me, so that the woman stirred in her sleep and called his name, and he was on his feet in an instant.

— What is it, Nella?

She said to him, why are you talking?

— You're dreaming, he said.

He bent down and kissed her and she made a little sound, of content and acknowledgment.

— Mevrou Vorster was here, before you came in.

— So you had a good chat, he said teasingly.

— Her son says you're the most wonderful officer in the whole police, except perhaps the captain. He's not sure which.

He laughed quietly.

— Out of his great experience, that's something, he said.

— And he says that down in the location you're a kind of god.

— Did he?

Then she turned over, awake.

— What's the matter with Dick?

— Why?

— It's not football, she said. It's some trouble.

And when he did not answer, she said, isn't it trouble? Or don't you want to tell me?

— It's trouble, he said. I don't mind telling you, but you wouldn't like to hear it.

— If you don't mind telling me, I don't mind hearing it.

— It would be in confidence, he said.

— Of course.

— I caught him.

She was now thoroughly awake, and half raised herself, leaning on her elbow.

— You caught him? Doing what?

— Chasing a girl.

— Dick! What girl?

And he looked at her in the darkness, and said with deliberation, a black girl.

And he could see in the darkness her shock and her revulsion. And she was silent until she said, to think he was in this house. And when she had thought of that, she said, will he be tried? It'll kill his mother. So he said to her gravely, I tried him. Then she considered that for a long time before she said, you forgave him.

— Yes.

— I'll not forgive him.

— You don't know about it, he said gently.

— You can't help but know about that, Pieter.

— Would you have killed his mother?

And that question she could not answer, for her gentleness was as great as her revulsion.

— Will you have him here again, she said.

He looked at her and said, not if I don't have to. But if I have to, I must, seeing I can't tell him that you know.

— All right, she said.

She stayed for some moments leaning on her elbow. Then she said, Goodnight, Pieter, and lay down. He bent over her and kissed her again, and got into his own bed. He had lain there some time, awake and thinking, and sure she was asleep, when suddenly she turned over and said to him, in the study, Pieter, not in our other rooms.

IV

And that was true, that to the black people in the location he was like a god. He was like a god to the black children on the farm where he was born, his father's farm, Buitenverwagting, which means Beyond Expectation. It lies on the edge of the grass country, and slopes down through a dozen kloofs into the country of Maduna, the reserve our forefathers gave to the black people when they subjugated them a hundred years gone by. There was for the black children nothing that he could not do. He could write and read, not one book, not a dozen books, but any book that he lifted up, which was a wonder to them all. He could read even the books they had in their own language, and the Bible translated by the English missionaries, and it was a wonder to hear their own tongue coming out of these black marks on white paper. It was our custom to allow our boys to play with the black boys, but not our girls with their girls. But after a certain age it stopped, not by law but by custom, and the growing white boy became the master.

It was not only this reading and writing, but the riding

and the shooting, and his grave self-confidence, that gave him his command over them. And his great height too, for at sixteen he was as tall as his father, who was six foot three. Both were just in their dealings with the black people, but the one's justice was stern and strict, and the other's gentle, though with a gentleness that allowed no disobedience or insolence. The black boys would take their disputes to him, and he would settle them this way or that, and they were at once all pleased and laughing, the winners laughing at the losers, and the losers at themselves.

His father would have punished sternly any familiarity between black and white, but the truth was that his son gave no excuse for such a thing. Sometimes I thought his father saw that too, that where he ruled by a strict and iron law, his son ruled by no law at all.

As he was to the black people of the farm, so he was to the location people in Venterspan. For now he was a man of authority in the police, second only to the captain, who was an austere man that never laughed or smiled that one could see. There was reason for that too, for though the captain never spoke of it, it was well known what had made him so. His only son had been crawling through a fence with a gun, as others had done before and do now and will do again, and had blown his head off; and his wife had died soon after, of a broken heart, they said. Now he lived with his mother in Venterspan, and never laughed or smiled. The captain was an Englishman, Massingham by name, but he spoke Afrikaans as we do ourselves, and of all the men of Venterspan he was the only one who spoke to my brother as man to man, for my brother had a great respect for austerity and silence, though he was no lover of Englishmen. And the girl Nella had a great respect for him also, and he an affection for her, which I never saw him show to any other person.

It was not long after this first event which I have written down, of the boy Dick, that my nephew went down to the location; and the *klonkies* there, the small black boys, having learned it from the soldiers who camped in Venterspan during the war of 1939, saluted him. They threw their bodies into a great stiffness, and some closed their eyes as though that gave them greater power to salute, so that a push would have sent them over. With the knowledge of children, they knew that he observed all these things, so that they put more vigour into them, relaxing when he had gone, and returning to their games.

He made his way to one of the poorest of the houses, built with sods from the veld, and covered with iron that had long since rusted and was full of holes. At the door sat the old woman Esther in the sun, the woman reputed to be a hundred, perhaps a hundred and twenty years old, and the only soul alive who had seen the first white trekkers to the grass country, though I think it only a woman's vanity.

The lieutenant greeted her, and she raised her shrunken arm in greeting.

— Where is Stephanie, he said.

She made no answer to him, but looked out of her smoke-reddened eyes, as though he had not spoken at all. He was patient with her, not only because he was by nature gentle, but because all men have respect for such an age, even when it is black.

— Esther, where is Stephanie, he said.

— I heard you, she said.

He laughed at that, and stood there enjoying the sun and

the air. When he thought she had had time enough, he said to her, although it was as yet only the middle of the morning, the sun will soon go down.

She approved of his jest and chuckled at it.

— She is gone, *my baas.*

— In two days she must be in the court, he said.

She stared into vacancy, whether occupied with this thought or with others, he could not say.

— In two days she must be in the court.

— I heard you, she said.

— If she is not there, she will not get two weeks this time, but three months maybe.

A flicker of interest showed in her eyes.

— And who will look after you?

She took her time over it.

— Who will look after you, Esther?

— Find the child, she said, then you will find Stephanie.

She closed her eyes, and for all he knew she was asleep. He left her, knowing that the girl was said to keep a child in the reserves, out beyond Bremerspan, in Maduna's country.

On his way back to the police-station, he called in to see Matthew Kaplan, the little Jew who owned the Southern Transvaal Trading, and who was the brother of Abraham Kaplan of the Royal Hotel. He and the Jew were friends, and the storekeeper came forward to the counter with smiles of pleasure.

— How are you, lieutenant?

— I'm well, Kappie. Anything new?

Kappie held up his hands.

— You must have known, he said.

He went into his little office at the far end of the counter. It was the untidiest office I ever saw, and I often reproached him with it, but he laughed at me. For we Afrikaners of Venterspan were not against the Jews, as they were in some other places, nor do we think that all shops should be in Afrikaners' hands. We never had any boycotts or secret plans against the Jews, and for that the credit must go to my brother, and to Dominee Stander of the great Church, for neither would countenance any hatred of the Jews. The dominee often reminded us that our great Book came from the Jews, and that we too were a people of Israel, who suffered and died to win the Holy Land; and this was the only book that my brother ever read.

Kappie came back from his dirty office with one of those envelopes that you can see through, that are used by dealers in stamps.

— Look at those, he said.

— Cape triangulars, Kappie. What did you pay?

Kappie took them out with a pair of what the English call tweezers, as if he were holding a baby, if you held a baby that way.

— Beautiful, eh? How much do you think, lieutenant.

— I've no idea, Kappie.

— Guess, lieutenant, guess.

— Twelve pounds.

Kappie was pleased by that.

— Thirty-two pounds, he said. Four pounds for a single, but thirty-two pounds for the block.

— Too much for me, Kappie.

— It's my only pleasure, said Kappie, as though sorry about his riches, for they said he was very rich, and wore old clothes and lived without a servant at the back of his shop, because all his money was going to his brother Abraham's daughter over at the Royal. She could make music come out of a violin like no other being that I ever heard, like the cries and lamentations of men and nations forsaken, rising and rising till you felt you could bear them no longer, and would die if they did not fall. Kappie told me it was the sufferings of the Jews that came out of her violin, and that I could believe, for many of our Afrikaner *liedjies* are the same, being filled with *heimwee* for places of home and birth, recalling the hurts of the past, and wakening deep longings for something known only to the Creator.

— But I have something else, said Kappie.

His face was alight with pleasure, and he brought out another envelope from his pocket. This envelope you could see through also, and in it were a pair of our own stamps, one in Afrikaans and one in English. They were not separated but still together, for which they have some foreign word of their own that I cannot now remember. And for some odd reason of their own it is more valuable to have them like that, and it makes them cost a lot more money. If you cannot understand it, I cannot explain it, never having understood it myself.

The lieutenant took the envelope and was as pleased as Kappie himself, and he said, Kappie, you're a wonder. How much now? And don't overcharge me.

— I pay for these triangulars, lieutenant, thirty-two pounds. I say to the dealer, I figure these two South Africans for a present. So I get them for a present.

The lieutenant said to him unwillingly, like a man feeling over-righteous, I can't take presents, Kappie.

Kappie was hurt.

— You are not a policeman to me, he said.

But when he saw that the lieutenant was unhappy, he said quickly, five shillings.

Then he said stubbornly, a customer can beat me down, but he cannot beat me up.

The lieutenant laughed.

— Done, he said.

Then suddenly Kappie put his own envelope into his pocket, and he said quickly to the lieutenant, put them away.

But the lieutenant did not understand him, not until he heard behind him the voice of his father in one of his hearty and joking moods.

— *Môre*, Kappie. *Môre*, Pieter. What are you up to there?

The lieutenant turned and saluted his father.

— Well, what are you up to?

The lieutenant held out the stamps. My brother looked at them, long enough to know they were stamps. Two giants looking at each other, one with a great stick that matched himself, the other with the small tweezers and the stamps. And the hearty and joking mood was gone.

— Kaplan, I've some business for you.

He took another short look at the stamps.

— I'll come back, he said, when . . . this other business is finished.

He walked heavily out of the store and into the street.

— I told you to put them away, lieutenant.

— I didn't understand you, Kappie.

Kappie shrugged his shoulders.

— Today he beats me in the business.

— Why, Kappie?

— When he calls me Kaplan, he always beats me in the business. When he calls me Kappie . . .

He shrugged his shoulders, and laughed.

— Then nobody wins in the business. These stamps make trouble, he said.

— There was trouble long before the stamps, said the lieutenant.

He looked at his friend.

— I was born before the stamps.

He picked up his stick.

— Thank you, Kappie.

He turned to go out of the store, but at the door Kappie caught up with him.

— Lieutenant.

— Yes.

— You were right about the present.

The lieutenant smiled, and his dark face was suddenly lit up, as though there were some lamp of the soul that turned off and on. When Kappie told me of it long after, I remembered the words of the book, the light of the body is the eye, and when the eye is true then is the body full of light, but when the eye is evil, then is the body dark. Darkness and light, how they fought for his soul, and the darkness destroyed him, the gentlest and bravest of men.

V

The lieutenant went out of the store and into van Onselen Street, with the black mood on him, thinking of the stamps. He was fourteen years old when my brother forbade him to go on with the stamps. It was the first time he had not come top in his class, and my brother told me to put the stamps away, because they were interfering with the boy's education. The boy was not sullen, he was never sullen. He stood there before his father, as though he could not believe what he heard, as though a great hurt were being done him that he had not deserved. And all the girl came out of him then, and looked out of his unbelieving eyes, that could not see how such a thing could be done.

— You may go, said my brother.

— Yes, father.

Where he went I do not know, somewhere on the farm, perhaps to the Long Kloof, which was his favourite of them all.

— The boy wasn't well, said my sister-in-law.

My brother looked at her out of his heavy eyes, then he turned to me.

— I said put them away, he said.

When the boy came back he was silent. That was the day when he first armoured himself, against hurts and the world, for to his mother and me he said never a word. He was a man before he spoke of it again, jokingly. I thought then he had got over it, but now I know I was wrong. It was simply a man that could now afford to come out from his armour, it being complete. When he was seventeen years old, he passed first-class in his Matriculation Examination, and we were all proud of him. After dinner when my brother had read from the great Bible that our ancestor Andries van Vlaanderen had brought from the Cape on the Great Trek of 1836, he prayed, and gave thanks to the Creator for the boy's success. When he finished, he said, Sophie, the stamps.

I remember now my foolishness. I made as if I did not understand what stamps, though I had thought of them each day of these three years. But my brother looked at me, and rebuked my pretence without words. What foolish things we do to cover ourselves, and by doing them are uncovered. I brought back the books of the stamps, wrapped up in a parcel, and put them in front of him. Then my brother made one of his jokes, one of the jokes that only he understood. I do not believe he meant to hurt. I think that if he meant to laugh at anything he meant to laugh at himself. I think even he was acknowledging a kind of defeat. I think the hurt in it was to hurt himself. But who can explain such things to a boy?

— Pieter, he said.

The boy went and stood before him, and said, Yes, father.

My brother smiled at him, a rare thing for him. And my sister-in-law and I, who understood him, knew that he was struggling to be kind, that kindness and sternness were struggling within him, so that the kindness came out all stern and struggling, confusing to a child.

— I thought I would get you a rifle, he said. Then I thought you would rather have the stamps.

The boy took the stamps, and made a little bow, and said, thank you, father. What my brother expected, I do not know. Did he think the boy would open them there, flushing with pleasure, and grateful? The boy sat down and put them on his knees, and whether by fear or constraint or hurt, I do not know, but he did nothing more at all. One did not often see my brother helpless, but he was helpless then, with a look that he tried to conceal, of bewilderment and anger and hurt. It was my sister-in-law who ended it. She rose and went to the boy and took up the parcel, and said to him, come with me. She took him to his room, and she who so seldom commanded, said, open it. He opened it, and there were his own books, with packets of stamps he had never seen before, that she and I had bought during the forbidden years, and all the new South Africans that he would have missed. Then he was moved and wept like a girl, and she comforted him, and they looked at the stamps. But he never brought them out again; he kept them always in his room. He never tired of counting them; he kept the totals in a book, and the dates opposite them. And if he got a new one, he would count them all again. If he reached a hundred mark, say eight hundred, he would put that and the date in big bold letters; when he reached the first thousand mark, he put that in big letters an inch high, and wrote after it PRESTASIE which means ACHIEVEMENT. But when he reached the two thousand, he must have thought it childish, for he blotted it out, but the thick dark letters could still be seen if you knew what they had been.

But they were never mentioned again in his father's presence, nor I think did his father ever forgive him for having humbled him; for by now each had a strange power over the other, which made certain quite ordinary things impossible to speak of any more. And each had a power over me too, and because of that power I was silent, when I should have cried out not ceasing.

So after his meeting with his father in Kappie's store, the lieutenant walked to the police-station in a mood dark and black, because his father had said, *when this other business is finished*, as though he were talking to boys. It was because of this mood that he humbled Sergeant Steyn, and turned his dislike into enmity, so that when the weapon was put into his hand, the sergeant struck the lieutenant down, and all of us with him. This thing I know because it was one of the things that he wrote when he was in prison.

He put his cap and his stick in his office, and when the sergeant called for him, went out to inspect the yard and the cells. It was a task he never enjoyed, for Steyn was a dour man, as the Scottish people say. When the war of 1939 burst on us, my nephew was in his first year in the Police, after taking his degree at Stellenbosch, and why he should join the Police I never knew. He took the red oath, which meant that he would go anywhere in Africa, and they gave him red flashes to put on his shoulders. But the red oath, to those who would not take it, meant only one thing, that the wearer of it was a Smuts man, a traitor to the language and struggle

of the Afrikaner people, and a lickspittle of the British
Empire and the English King, fighting in an English war
that no true Afrikaner would take part in. So some wore
the flashes of the red oath, and some wore none, and this
caused great bitterness in the Police, and great division
amongst our people. And divisions in families too, even our
own, for my brother said it was an English war, and would
not believe the stories of Hitler and the Jews; but his wife
and I were for the English, as we have always been in our
hearts, since Louis Botha and Jan Smuts made us so. Then
when Holland was invaded and Rotterdam destroyed . . .
but let that wait.

The boy was a great soldier in the war, as I knew
he would be; he won the Distinguished Service Order
and came back with a great row of medals, which my
brother called *uitheemse kaf*, which means foreign trash,
on his breast. They made him a major when he was twenty-
four, and when he came back with that, what could they do
but make him an officer in the Police. But Sergeant Steyn
would not take the red oath, holding like my brother that
it was an English war; and then he found himself, an older
man, with a young man over him, lieutenant because he had
been to the war.

During these inspections the lieutenant and the sergeant
never exchanged a word such as human beings might have
exchanged with each other. Once when the sergeant's wife
was ill, and my nephew had enquired after her, the sergeant,
polite and correct, had answered so that my nephew could
never ask again. Almost as if he had said, my private life is my
own. And on top of that was the dark black mood, brought
on by the foolish stamps.

The sergeant opened the cells for him, and in the corner by the jamb of one of the doors were some seeds of maize, used for the feeding of native prisoners who were waiting for the court, and who if sentenced, would be sent to prison.

And the lieutenant said, what are those?

The sergeant went red as a boy, and would have bent down to pick them up, but the lieutenant was in the way. The sergeant looked at him as though he might move, but the lieutenant did not move. Then the sergeant said stiffly, seeds of maize.

Then he said, shall I pick them up, lieutenant?

But the lieutenant said to him, with the black gall in his heart, it's not your work to pick up seeds of maize, get the man whose work it is.

— He's drawing clothes, lieutenant. He's wanted in court.

So the lieutenant stooped and picked up the seeds of maize. The sergeant made a move to take them, but the lieutenant gave no attention to him, and walked himself to the garbage can, with a face of stone. He lifted the lid and threw the seeds in. Then he looked at the lid, at every part of the lid. Then he looked at every part of the can. Then he said with a fine and useless justice, they're clean.

Then something of his father came into him, and he said, I ought to know, it was my first work in the army.

Then he finished his inspection, but by this time he was ashamed, and if he saw anything to speak of, he said not a word. He walked out of the yard and into his office, and sat there at his work, trying to get the foolish matter out of his mind.

He was not long at his work before the captain came in, and he stood up at once. He and the captain always spoke in

English, and why I cannot say; but it is so that when two men speak both our languages, they usually speak to each other only in the one, except perhaps when a third man is present, and they speak in the one that he knows the best.

— Good morning, sir.

— Good morning, van Vlaanderen. Sit down.

My nephew sat down, and the captain went and stood by the window, and looked out into the yard.

— What's the matter with Steyn, he said.

And when the lieutenant had told him, he said, were you severe?

— I didn't think so, sir.

— A word from you is twice as severe because it comes from you.

Because the lieutenant did not answer, he said, do you know that?

And after a pause the lieutenant said, I know what you mean, sir.

— Therefore, said the captain, you could say half what you mean.

Then he said, to an older man, perhaps nothing at all.

The lieutenant stood up again.

— I'm sorry, sir, he said.

— I'm not reprimanding you, said the captain; I'm telling you.

He left the window and walked to the table.

— You'll go far, he said, farther than I ever will. Perhaps as far as can be gone. But you don't need to do anything about it. It'll come to you.

— You understand, he said, Steyn didn't speak to me. It was just something that I saw.

— I understand, sir.

— What about the girl Stephanie?

The lieutenant told him.

— Go down tomorrow, said the captain. You can have young Vorster and one of the native constables.

Then he walked from the table to the door.

— Did you hear about Smith, he asked.

— No, sir.

— Coetzee phoned from Sonop; he was sentenced this morning.

— To what, sir?

— Death.

The two men stood there in a kind of heavy silence, as men stand in the presence of the name of death, neither looking at the other.

— And the wife, sir?

— A year.

Unsmiling the captain went out. And the lieutenant said to himself, God have mercy upon him, Lord Jesus have mercy upon him. And again he said, God have mercy upon me, Lord Jesus have mercy upon me.

VI

So Smith received the sentence of death. None of our family knew the man Smith, but we knew people who had, and they all said the same, that he was just an ordinary man, quiet and inoffensive, who had little schooling and no great brains, and worked hard on a small and poor farm down towards Swaziland, and remote from the world. So here was someone who was known by someone you knew, and was given the sentence of death.

His case was talked about privately, not before children or servants, not even before people in a room. If two men were talking about it in the street, they would do it in low voices; and if another joined them, even a friend, they might well talk at once of something else. A man might sit at his table with his grown-up family, and put down the newspaper angrily, and say in a strained voice, he must be hanged; they would all know what he meant, but they would not talk about it, they would let it rest. My brother would read about it, with a face of anger and revulsion, but he never talked about it to my sister-in-law or to me. Nella van Vlaanderen would neither read nor talk about it at all, and there were many women like her, as if by reading of it they would acknowledge that such things happened in the world. Others would read the newspaper in private, hiding their reading from others, attracted and repelled by its horror, ashamed of themselves and of a world where such things happened. As for jesting, there was hardly a man, and certainly no woman, who would jest about it, not even those who liked their jesting coarse and rough.

For Smith, while his wife was with child, made also with child the black servant girl in the house. When she told him she was with child, he was filled with terror, and could think of nothing else by night or by day, nor did he touch her any more. So great was his fear, that either he told his wife or she read it in his face, or the girl told her. And so great was her own fear, or so did he impart his own to her, that they agreed to add to the terror, and planned the girl's death. By night they took her to a river, and having drowned her, cut off her head, and buried it so that no one should know who it was, and the body they sank in the river with weights. Then they gave it out that the girl was run away, and got another.

But the girl's father would not believe that she had run away, for she had been of a quiet and obedient nature; nor would he and the girl's mother have opposed her wishes had she wished to marry some man, nor would they have been harsh and unforgiving had she been found with child. Days passed, and there was no news of her. Smith and his wife, who lived already in a second terror greater than the first, having done that which they had never thought of all their lives, passed under a third and yet greater terror when the police said to them, it looks like murder.

No one would have murdered the girl out of greed, for she had nothing; nor out of jealousy, for she had no lovers; nor out of anger, for she was submissive and gentle by nature. Therefore it was done from fear. And if a man of her own race and colour had made her with child, he would not have been afraid and murdered her, but would have gone shamefaced to her father, to confess and make reparation, as was their custom. Therefore it was a white man; and who, in that lonely and deserted place, but the man who was her master? So Smith and his wife passed under the last and greatest terror of them all, when the police came looking about the farm.

On the second day they found blood, on one of the blades of the hundred blades of a hummock of grass, one of the thousands, the ten thousands of hummocks on the farm. On the third day they found the head of the girl, on the fourth her body; then they knew she had been with child. Smith, a religious man after his own fashion, and if doubtful of the love of God, assured of His wrath, confessed, and his wife with him; and the great machinery of the law, having found him, turned to its task of retribution.

This was the case that men talked about in low voices, in every town and on every farm of the grass country, and in many another place in South Africa. And in the locations of the black people, and in the servants' rooms, they talked about it also, with anger and horror, and with a certain wonder and awe of this sudden manifestation of the certitude and majesty of the white man's law.

And I? Let me write it without fear, being now beyond loss. It was said by our Lord and Saviour Jesus Christ, lo of old it was said to you, an eye for an eye, and a tooth for a tooth, but I say to you, use not force against an evil man. And it was said by Him also, when He hung suffering on the cross, Father, forgive them, for they know not what they do. And again it was said by Him, judge not that ye be not judged. And yet again, whosoever offends one of these little ones (and I take it this is true of one unborn), it were better that a millstone were hung round his neck, and he were thrown into the sea. And the Apostle Paulus wrote to the Romans, let everyone put himself under the magistrates, because there is no power that is not from God, and all powers are ordered by Him.

Therefore my mind was confused, but I am one of a people who in this matter of white and black suffer no confusion. Therefore I said to myself, what indeed many others said, what even I believe my brother would have said, let the man be hanged and the woman go free. For my brother believed as the Apostle Paulus, that the husband is the head of the wife, and that her true nature is to be obedient; which thing indeed he practised in his own house. Yet I grieved for the man in my heart, that did such evil because he was in terror.

*　　*　　*　　*　　*

And the captain was restless in his mind, and came back to the lieutenant's office, telling him to go on with his work, and standing about there, looking out of the window, and saying nothing.

Then at last he spoke.

— God knows, he said, I don't.

And went out again.

And the lieutenant sat at his desk, looking at his papers

and seeing nothing, and saying over and over in his heart, *God wees my genadig, o Here Jesus wees my genadig.*

The telephone rang, and it was his mother.

— Son, what happened this morning?

He knew her face was full of care and apprehension, and he answered her light-heartedly.

— Ah, I was caught, he said. Redhanded.

— He told me about it.

— Did he?

— Yes, and that's strange. He said he went up to you, determined to be friendly. But when he saw the stamps the devil came into him. Why should he tell me such a thing?

— I don't know, mother.

— Perhaps he meant me to tell you, Pieter.

— Perhaps he did.

— Don't take it seriously, son.

— Mother, he treated us like children.

— Son, she said, don't take it seriously.

— All right, mother.

— Here's Tante Sophie, she said.

Then I said to him, you won't forget his birthday?

— As if I would dare. What shall I get him? A pipe?

— Can't you forget about the pipe, I said. It wasn't because it was from you. He just didn't like it.

— I'm getting him a book, he said.

— You're joking, Pieter.

For we all knew that he read only one Book.

— I've got it already, he said.

— What is it?

— *The Life of General Smuts*, he said.

— Now I know you're joking.

— Wait and see, he said.

He put down the telephone, and said to himself in English, be damned to the stamps. He settled down to his papers, but now he was thinking about the pipe. So it was just that his father didn't like the pipe? They knew as well as he, when the family was there together, and the pipe there in the rack for all to see, that not one of them would have dared to say to him, Father, you've never smoked Pieter's pipe.

He went through the work of the day grimly, and at five o'clock came out into the street. When he had no wish to talk, none could avoid it better than he. No one would have dared to break into his abstraction, for the honour in which he was held was of fear as well as affection. That is why many said that he would be the captain of the Springboks, because of the strange authority that he had over men.

When he reached his home, Nella brought him coffee, and a new biscuit that she was trying.

— How is it, she asked.

— It's good, he said.

He ate some more of it, like some judge at a show.

— But not so good as your last.

He could hear the children splashing in the bath, and he finished the coffee and biscuit, and got up to go to them. But before he reached the door, Nella spoke to him; he saw she was not looking at him, and he was filled with irritable resignation.

— Yes.

— What's the matter with you, Pieter?

She spoke in a low voice, which he gloomily supposed was a mark of tragedy.

— Why ask, he said lightly. Is it because I didn't like the biscuit?

— It's nothing to do with the biscuit, she said.

— It's because I don't talk.

— That's only part of it, she said.

— I've told you that after a day's work I don't feel like talking. I want to be quiet.

— You'll be quiet all evening, she said. Unless someone comes to talk football. And even they don't come so often. We might be in the desert.

He looked at her helplessly.

— Sometimes I wish that I were a stamp, she said. Then you might look at me.

The mention of the stamps angered him. He suddenly thought of van Belkum, the school teacher, who never stopped talking, who talked all day in school and talked all night at home, about nothing at all, about the weather, and the aeroplane that had crashed in India, and whether a big family was better than a small family, and the rising prices, and the Ford versus the Chevrolet, and the bad and good points of the Jews, and the misery of cancer, and the car that was stolen outside his very house.

— You should have married van Belkum, he said. Then you could have talked.

— It's not the talking, she said. It's you, your mood.

— What mood?

— Your black mood.

He laughed without mirth.

— I haven't a black mood, he said.

— Black, she said, black. You weren't like that when you were younger.

— No one was.

— You evade me.

— You evade me too, he said.

She seemed to have finished speaking, she did not look at him, he knew there would be tears in her eyes. For one moment he thought he would comfort her, but rebelled against it.

— I'll go to the children, he said. They don't know about my moods.

She turned quickly, and sure enough there were tears in her eyes.

— That's true, she said. I often envy them.

— They give something to me, he said angrily. That's my nature. I give when I'm given.

She turned back to face the table.

— I can't go over it all again, she said.

He said to her urgently, childishly, one day you'll regret it.

With that threat he left her, and went to the bathroom. The small boy called to him.

— I'm ready, father.

He put the towel round the small body, and lifted it up, and pressed it against his own, and pressed the small wet cheek against his cheek, with fierce gentleness, as though the warm flesh could assuage the pain of his moods and angers, the whole misery that he himself hated and could not understand.

Ag, he wanted from the girl what she could not give, for all her lovingness. For he was the one that was like a god, not she. He was the one that had read all the books, and had been up and down the continent of Africa, and in Italy and

England, and had flown in the air and sailed on the sea. He was the one that had commanded men, and seen them kill and being killed. He was the one that had had the great crowds clapping him, and had received praise and honours. But she was the country girl, quiet and shy and chaste, as most of our country girls are. She was frightened of Johannesburg, and of the evil things that men and women do, even of staying in an hotel. She was frightened even of of the laughter that came out of the Royal Bar, where men like her father and brothers were jesting a little coarse and rough. Therefore when he in his extremity asked for more of her love, she shrank from him, thinking it was the coarseness of a man. Then the hard hand of Fate struck her across the face, and shocked her into knowledge, but only after we had been destroyed.

VII

It was a perfect day when the lieutenant went to look for Stephanie. It had rained in the night, and the grass country was green and fresh, with the cool wind blowing, and the grass-larks calling from the veld. The red road was firm after the rain, and there was no dust to spoil the freshness of the day, or the cleanness of the grass country, or the purity of the great bowl of the sky, with the white clouds floating. It was the kind of country where he was born, that he had roamed over as a boy, after the partridge and the wild duck on the pans. Young Vorster, who was driving, who thought there was no man like him except perhaps the captain, saw the lieutenant grow back into the boy, and heard him saying, not once or twice but many times, this is the country, this is the country. The lieutenant sat, not back in repose, but forward in eagerness, drinking in the air and the wide expanse, talking more than the young constable had ever heard him talk before. He pointed out the homesteads of the farms, saying who lived in them, and how many *morgen* they had there, and what the grown-up children were doing now. And if the homestead could not be seen, for the farms are rich and large in the grass country, he would say where it lay, and what trees grew there, and that there was a girl there, lovely and true, who would make a good wife for a young constable, and might one day bring him riches, so that he could give up the Police, and ride round in the sun and air. And what was better than that, for in the rain you could hear the plovers calling, and the *piet-my-vrou* would cry from the kloof, which was like a hand suddenly plucking at the strings of the heart, so that your whole being shook and trembled; and why and why, why no one knew, it was the nature of man and of creation, that some sound, long remembered from the days of innocence before the world's corruption, could open the door of the soul, flooding it with a sudden knowledge of the sadness and terror and beauty of man's home and the earth. But you could not keep such knowledge, you could not hold it in your hand like a flower or a book, for it came and went like the wind; and the door of the soul would not stay open, for maybe it was too great joy and sorrow for a man, and meant only for angels. Yet you could ride again in the rain, in the *piet-my-vrou's* season, and he would call again, and catch you again by the throat and make you tremble.

Then the lieutenant was silent, exhausted by the rush of words, and a little constrained; and he said in an ordinary voice, as if to sum it all up and wipe it all out together, as though it were really something of no real account, that's what a sound can do to you.

— I had a sound too, said the young constable.

His face and voice were eager, so the lieutenant had to overcome his constraint, seeing it was he himself who had made the young man eager.

— You had a sound too?

— Yes, said the young constable, when my mother used to open the big tin in the pantry.

Then the lieutenant exploded with laughter, and looked to see if the young constable were hurt, but he was not hurt at all, for the lieutenant's poetry and laughter were music alike to him.

After they had visited the police post at Bremerspan, they left the road that runs south to Natal and Zululand, and turned to the east, by the rough track that goes down into the reserve which our forefathers gave to Maduna when he yielded to them, a hundred years ago. The track was steep in places, for the grass country falls down steeply into the low country.

Here the black people lived their lives in a separate world, in the round grass huts with their small fields of maize and beans and sweet potatoes. Some say it would be better if they stayed there altogether, for then they would be protected against the evils of our civilisation; but the truth is they cannot stay there, for their small fields cannot keep them, and they must come out to work for food and clothes. They go in their thousands to Johannesburg and Durban, nearly all the men, and every young man and woman, and there learn many new things, so that some never come back, and some come back with new ideas never before thought of in the low country.

Their old respect for the white people is passing away, and if the father put down his hat at the door before he came into your house, the son will hold it in his hand, causing some to say that the grandson will keep it on his head. But that I do not believe.

Yet though this so-called separate world has so been changed by us, though the English missionaries are there with their school and hospital, though so many of its able-bodied men and so many of its young women are away, though the brave tribal dress gives way more and more to white people's cast-off clothes, though Maduna's great-great-grandson has a motor-car, yet it is a separate world all the same, and of its joys and sorrows no one knows at all.

But the Police knew it well, not so much because it was lawless, but because they often found some person there who was being looked for by the Police in Johannesburg.

The lieutenant reached this country at about noon, and leaving the car, made for the huts where the girl Stephanie was reported to keep her child, and there an old man, dressed in an old greatcoat, such as they wore in the army, came out at the sound of them.

— *Môre, my baas. Môre, my baas.*

— We are looking for the girl Stephanie, said the lieutenant.

The old man looked down at his greatcoat and adjusted it, though there was no need to adjust it. Then he frowned as though compelling himself to great effort in the interests of law and justice.

— Stephanie, he said, Stephanie.

The lieutenant smiled, not purposely, but as one smiles at such acting, knowing it is acting, but enjoying it. And the man, seeing the smile and knowing its meaning, was at once in its power. But he shook his head with a kind of sorrow, and said, Stephanie. And the lieutenant, as if agreeing with him, said also, Stephanie. Then the old man spoke to the native constable in their own language.

— I know this girl Stephanie, he said.

And though the lieutenant knew this language, the native constable said to him in Afrikaans, he says he knows the girl Stephanie. So to humour the old man, the lieutenant said to the native constable in Afrikaans, where is she now?

The two black men spoke again, and the native constable said in Afrikaans, he says she lives in the dorp. The lieutenant smiled again, and seeing him again, the old man was still more in his power, especially when the white man put the slight note of authority into his voice, and said, I am waiting.

The two black men spoke again, and the native constable said, he says it is a difficult matter, but the lieutenant took no notice of him, but looked at some other place, to show that he was waiting.

— He asks a favour.

— Yes.

— He asks you not to go straight to the place he will tell us, but to go first to some of the other huts. The lieutenant nodded, and he and the young constable walked away, one to one hut, and the other to another. Then the native constable walked to yet another, and when they met again, he told the lieutenant, not pointing but nodding his head, that the girl was in one of the kloofs in the hills, where they sloped steeply back into the grass country, and up to the farms of the white people. The kloof was wooded, not with forest, but with what we in South Africa call the bush, and trees grow there because the hills catch the wet winds from the distant sea.

— He does not know if she is still there, said the native

constable, for if you climb out at the top of it, you could
go to many other places and not be seen. But she went there
when she heard we were coming.

— So she heard we were coming.

— Yes, *meneer.*

— You and Maseko go up the small kloof, said the lieutenant, and when I see you come out at the top, I'll start
up the big one.

They set off, and he sat down on the ground and lit his
pipe, enjoying the sun and the freedom. For at Buitenverwagting, where he was born, the hills ran down with kloofs
like these to the low country, to the reserve of Maduna. He
knew them all, and the trees and the ferns and flowers, the
sharp-tasting water plant that children chewed for its sour
juice, and the magic never known again, save in memory,
for duty and law and custom closed on you, and work too,
and you did what thousands had done before you and
thousands would do after you, so that something could con-
tinue that had no magic or wonder at all.

The black boys came to watch him as he sat there.
Some sat on the ground too, as though they would sit there
as long as he. They talked quietly amongst themselves,
about his business here and the soldier's ribbons that he
wore, so that he smiled to himself, and they seeing it knew
that he understood them, and said that also. And if there
had been time for it, he would have had the power over them
too, and they would have done anything that he required,
and found it pleasure. But he rose suddenly, for he had seen
the two men come out at the top of the kloof. The boys
scattered at once, observing his great height with wonder.
He walked past them, giving them a small salute in return

for their greetings, which greatly pleased them. He chose
a path that seemed to lead to the big kloof, and walked
along it through the fields of maize, and the weeds of old
fields lying fallow. His choice was right, for the path suddenly turned, and in a moment he was in the bush, where
the *singsingetjie,* the shrill cicada, made its piercing song in
the coolness. Here was what lay in the store of memory, the
water running over the stones and the sharp-tasting water
plants and the mosses and ferns. Then suddenly ahead of
him, under a little fall of water, he saw the girl Stephanie.

When he was near her, she turned and looked at him,
smiling the secret smile, and then submissively turned her
eyes to the ground.

— Stephanie.

— Yes, *baas.*

— What are you doing here?

— I came to see my child, she said.

— Here? In the kloof?

She smiled sheepishly.

— Down there, she said, where you were.

— Why didn't you ask me if you could come?

She looked to left and right, taking her time.

— I thought the *baas* would say no.

— And tomorrow you must be in the court.

— I would have been there, she said.

— How?

— I would have walked.

— Now you can ride, he said.

But seemingly she did not want to ride, for suddenly she
had fled by a little path at the side of the fall, that came to
another, with no way up except over the rocks of the fall

itself, green and slippery. He followed her at leisure, and came to where she was standing.

— Why did you do that, he asked.

She made him no answer, except to smile in her strange and secret way. Then she heard the sound of the men above, and drew back. And as she drew back she touched him. And he did not move.

He did not move, neither forward nor back, nor did she. It was all silent but for the sounds of the men above, and for his breathing, and the racing of his heart. Then she turned round and smiled at him again, briefly, and moved forward an inch or two, standing still with her eyes on the ground; while he, shaking with shame, went and sat on a stone, and took off his cap and wiped his brow, hot and cold and trembling. She did not turn to look at him, but went on smiling, with her eyes on the ground. Above them the sounds of the descending men grew nearer and louder. She lifted her head and looked upwards into the kloof, waiting for them with a kind of forlorn enjoyment.

Then Vorster called out, are you there, lieutenant?

— I'm here, called the lieutenant, the girl's here too.

— *Baas.*

— Yes.

— Can I see the child before I go?

— Yes.

The smile of irresponsibility left her face, changing it and surprising him.

— *Dis my enigste kind,* it's my only child, she said.

She was filled with some hurt pride of possession, so that he, knowing her life, wondered at it.

— It's my only child, she said, and looked down at the

ground again, waiting hopelessly. He, feeling pity for her, was suddenly purged of the sickness of his mind, and stood up and put on his cap.

— That was a good plan, lieutenant, said the young constable from the top of the fall. He looked for a place to land, and jumped like a cat, softly and easily.

— I could do that once, said the lieutenant.

Vorster smiled disbelievingly, not that the lieutenant could have done it once, but at the implication that he could not do it now. The lieutenant signed to Maseko to lead the way down the kloof.

— You, Stephanie, he said.

She smiled, but not at him, and followed obedient, and Vorster followed her.

*   *   *   *   *

I waited till they had passed out of sight, and then I took off my cap and said, o God wees my genadig, o Here Jesus wees my genadig.

I did not expect any voice to answer, yet if a voice had answered me, I would have believed in it. If some voice had spoken to me there, out of the sky or the kloof or the trees about me, or if some new strength had come into me there, or if I had felt again as I felt in the days of my innocence, I would have believed in it. Yet I did not expect any voice to answer; that was the truth of it.

Then I thought of Nella and the children, with sudden realisation as though I had just seen myself, in a blinding light that exposed me. If it shocked me to see myself, it shocked me no less to see my danger. It was like a kind of shadow of myself, that moved with me constantly, but always apart from me; I knew it was there, but I had known it so long that it did not trouble me, so long as it stayed apart. But when the mad sickness came on me, it would suddenly move nearer to me, and I knew it would strike me down if it could, and I did not care. It was only when the sickness had passed that I saw how terrible was my danger, and how terrible too my sickness, that when it was on me my wife and children could be struck down, and I would not care.

I was suddenly filled with love for them, and longed to see them again and to touch them, as soon as I could. I put on my cap and went hurrying down the kloof after the others.

VIII

This was the time that Japie Grobler came to Venter-span, when they opened the new office of the Social Welfare Department. And because they had no other place for it, they opened it in the old butcher shop. It was a queer place for Social Welfare, for it still had the beam from which butchers hang their meat. Nothing could have suited Japie better, for it gave him a lot of new jokes, and he was a man who when he had a joke, brought it out whenever he could. He never troubled to remember the people he told it to, so that he would tell you the same joke two or three times and not know. He went to Matthew Kaplan and begged from him one of the hooks from the new butcher's shop, and he put the hook on the beam, right there in the middle of the office. He would be seeing some person in his office and making notes on paper, then he would suddenly stand up and go and put the piece of paper on the hook, and say seriously, that hook is for *hangende sake,* which is in English *pending cases,* and then he would roar with laughter. He tried his joke on the Dominee, who is a sober man and who

brought a case to him which he took soberly and earnestly.
And Japie roared with laughter, but the Dominee did not
laugh at all. Then Japie felt a fool and always after felt a
fool in the presence of the Dominee. When he roared with
laughter you could hear it in the street, and in Kaplan's
store, and even at the Service Station, so that the Venterspan
people must have thought that Social Welfare was a joking
business. My brother, having heard the story of the hook
already went more than once with some friend into the
office, and then he would ask Japie what the hook was for,
and Japie would tell him again, and roar with laughter;
my brother would laugh too, and the friend also, but at
the joker, not the joke. But at the second visit Japie saw
through the whole childish business, and was reluctant to
tell the joke at all. Then my brother would put on the manner that made people a little afraid of him, and say, Mr.
Social Welfare Officer, why do you have that hook? So
Japie would have to tell the joke again, feeling like a fool.
After that he grew shy, and told the girl in the office to
warn him when the *Oubaas* was coming, so that he could
slip out through the back door and do Social Welfare among
the weeds till my brother was safely by.

The Social Welfare Office came to Venterspan because
of our Women's Welfare Society, which we had set up about
a year before, to deal with the cases of the poor, and of
naughty and neglected children, not only of the poorer white
people, but also with the small *klonkies* from the black
people's location, who liked to hang round the store and
the Service Station, and round the place of the buses, where
they offered to carry the white people's things, and sooner
or later would take something that they had no right to. It

was my sister-in-law who made it so that we would look
after black as well as white children. She even had a committee of the black people in the location and would go down
and sit at the same table with them there in one of the
houses, and they all smiling and pleased, though of course
she would not have sat with them in the town. This is not
a thing that would be done by all Afrikaner women, and I
tell you it to show that my sister-in-law, for all that she was
full of care, had a strength of her own; and my brother
would treat her doings with a kind of growling, like a lion
growls, and you do not know if it is pleased or otherwise.
For she was a lover of the Lord Jesus Christ, and like Him
she was gentle and pure, and took to her heart His saying
that all children should be suffered to come unto Him. She
was the President of the Welfare Committee, and was loved
and respected for herself, and not only because she was the
wife of my brother. It was she who got my brother to go to
Pretoria and ask the Government for the Welfare Office, so
he went and got it; and he liked to say frowning, *it took
me thirty minutes*. For my brother was Chairman of the
whole Party in the grass country, and though he never went
to Parliament in Cape Town, being as halt and lame in
public speech as he was in walking, yet he ruled the Party
as he ruled his own home, and said that the Members of
Parliament were his span of oxen, though that was a joke
he made only privately.

Now Japie was also a boy of the grass country, and had
grown up with them all. He was of the same age as my
elder nephew, and they were deep friends in a way; but only
in a way, for one was tall and grave, and the other short and
full of jokes. They went together to school and university,

and Japie had the open door at Buitenverwagting and was
like a child of the house; and he and Pieter and Frans were
like brothers together. Indeed there was a time when we
thought he might have become their brother-in-law, but
that was not to be, for the moment we began to think it he
was away like a frightened bird; and soon after that his
people moved away, far beyond Sonop, to the farm Gena-
dendal, which is the Valley of Mercy.

Therefore I was surprised when I passed the place of
the busses, to see him there with his suitcases looking pleased
to be in the grass country. Then he saw me and rushed at
me, calling me not Tante Sophie but Ta' Sophie, which is
a thing I have never liked, it being a silly habit from the
Cape. He caught me by the arms and kissed me on both
cheeks, and looked at me as though I were his mother, which
is a deep pleasure for a woman like myself.

— What are you doing here, he said.

— What do you think, I said.

I looked at my shopping bag, and at my clothes, which
were such as you wear in your own town that has only one
street.

— Have you left Buitenverwagting, he asked.

— Yes.

— Why? Who's there?

— Quiet, man, I said, for he was still holding me and
shaking me about. We left because of the *Oubaas's* leg.

— I heard about his leg, he said. And how is the *Oubaas*?
And Ta' Mina?

— The *Oubaas* is well, I said sharply. And I said very
sharply, and clearly so he could hear me, Tante Mina is
well too.

— And who's at Buitenverwagting?

— Frans is there, I said. But why are you here? **Have** you left Social Welfare?

Then I suddenly understood, and I laughed too, to think that Japie Grobler was what my brother had got for going all the way to Pretoria.

He took his hands away from me, and put on what he thought was a proud and noble look.

— *I* can't leave Social Welfare, he said. I *am* Social Welfare. I'm the new Social Welfare Officer for Venterspan, Bremerspan, Sonop, Rusfontein . . . oh about ten places, wait a bit, it's all down on paper.

He took out one of those long envelopes that is marked On His Majesty's Service, though I hear the Government will change all that.

— Keep your paper, I said. They've put you in the butcher's shop.

His face fell a bit, but he recovered himself and said, I asked for a butcher's shop.

— Why, I said.

— So that I can make mincemeat of all the social problems of the grass country.

He roared with laughter, like a man suddenly attacked by some new disease, so that all the people in the street, white and black, looked at us.

— Stop your fooling, I said.

— Seeing you won't read the letter, he said, I'll tell you what they said to me privately. They said they wanted a man who will be held in respect by all, but won't knuckle down to the *predikants* and the Members of Parliament and the rich farmers, but will reform all the *klonkies* in the loca-

tion, and will uplift the whole district and maintain the
ideals of our forefathers and

— Don't think you'll run the Social Welfare Office, I said.
The *Oubaas* will run it.

Then he was serious again, and I wondered what was
coming.

— I jumped for joy when they told me I was coming, he
said; I thought, now I'll see old Pieter again.

He touched me, right in my heart, there in the middle
of van Onselen Street. Then he took me again by the arms,
and said to me gently, Ta' Sophie, Ta' Sophie.

— Don't Ta' Sophie me, I said.

I looked up the street, to hide myself from him, and
my eyes, and I said to him, don't think you've come to play
the fool in the Social Welfare Office.

He roared with laughter, and all the people turned to
look at us again, which I least of all desired.

— Must you laugh like that, I asked.

— That laugh will be respected here, he said. When they
hear it, people will say, you hear that, that's the man who
reformed the grass country.

— You're a fool, I said. I've got no time for fooling.
You'll come round soon?

— This very day, he said.

He called to one of the *klonkies* that were hanging about,
and he told him to carry the suitcases and I said to him,
that's what we got you here for, to stop things like that.

— I'm not in the office yet, he said.

So I left him there with his luggage, and went on, not
sure whether to be sorry or pleased that Japie Grobler was
our Social Welfare Officer, but glad that he had come to

Venterspan. Ah, if he could have bound the other to him, and brought out the laughter from that dark unhappy face, for there was laughter enough there, if one could have brought it out. And laughter heals mankind and makes the darkness light and eases pain; and it makes the eyes light up, and the soul throw off its heaviness, and sends the blood quicker through the veins, so that it casts out its evil humours. Ay, if he could have laughed and come again amongst us; but as his burden was his own, so was his happiness to sit silent in the veld, moved by some lonely joy. Child, child, would to God I could have died for you, would to God I had stayed hammering on the door, and cried out not ceasing. Would to God my love had had some power greater than your coldness, some flame that would have set the walls of your heart on fire, so that I could have come at you. And Japie, poor cheerful fool, went laughing through the town and the grass country, and tinkered in his merry way with this problem and that, and saw nothing of the greatest of them all.

Then I went to the court for our Women's Welfare Society, to hear the case of the girl Stephanie.

IX

My nephew was in the court when I got there, and that was a pleasant surprise to me, for he is not always there. He was also surprised to see me, and smiled at me with pleasure. He would not let me sit in the public seats, but took my arm, and led me to the seat next to himself, and I was proud to be led by a tall strong man, who was blood of my blood and of the same name as myself, and held in respect in this place. And I felt as I did on the day that Louis Botha left the great people that he was speaking to, and came over to me and took my hand in both his hands and said to me, your letter lifted me up when I was down. Which words I have never forgotten, because they are written in my heart.

The magistrate was not yet in, and I said to him, I've just met the new Social Welfare Officer.

— Who is it, Tante?

— You must guess, I said.

— Someone I know?

— As well as you know your own brother.

He thought for a minute, and then he said, well, well. Then he grinned at me and said, Father will be pleased.

For I must tell you that my brother, though he had a great fondness for Japie, thought he was a clown.

— Who is it, I said.

Then he grinned at me again.

— Don't be silly, he said.

But I insisted and so he humoured me.

— Japie, of course.

I was disappointed that he had guessed so easily.

— I could see he was a bit cast down to have to go into the butcher's shop, I said, but he said to me, I myself chose the butcher's shop.

— Why, Tante?

I told him and he laughed aloud.

— Pieter, why don't you laugh more often?

— You're after me again, he said. Quiet, the case is beginning.

They brought in the girl Stephanie, and then the magistrate came in, and we all stood up, and when he had sat down, we sat down again, but the girl stood in the dock, smiling her secret smile. Then she would think it not right to smile, or perhaps her smile had some time angered someone in authority, for she would frown as though by that she would show respect for the law and the court, and would show that she was not careless and indifferent. So she went between smiling and frowning, so that unseeing persons might not have known that that was the sign of her nervousness, and might not have believed it had they been told, thinking that she must by now surely be used to being in the court.

The magistrate found her guilty for the liquor, and indeed she herself pleaded so, but he decided that there was no proof that she had meant to run away from Venterspan nor any proof that she did not mean to return. He gave her the usual two weeks, which she received as she received other things, not with resentment or sullenness, but with the smile and the frown, and with the strange innocence that made me pity her, though innocent she could hardly be.

She was about to leave the court, and I thought that the magistrate had forgotten the matter of the child, but he suddenly held up his hand.

— You have a child, he said.

At the mention of the child, she was immediately another woman, and she looked round the court with wary eyes, as an animal might look round when it is hunted.

Then she said, I have a child.

— And you are always in prison?

— Not always, she said.

— How often have you been in prison?

She tried to count the times, even using her fingers, and smiled and frowned, but at last shook her head and gave it up.

— Many times?

— Yes, many times.

Then she said urgently, but not so many.

The magistrate wrote it down, and then he read it out, not always, but many times, but not so many.

She could see it was a jest, and that the magistrate and others were amused by it, and she looked round the court as if to be on guard the better. Then she saw that the magistrate was waiting, so she nodded her head, and looked again round the court.

— And you do not work?

— I cannot work, she said. The old woman is very old.

— Would not some other woman watch her while you went to work?

Yes, that is what they did, asked questions that grew harder and harder, leading you to a place where you could not escape.

— Would that not be possible?

— Yes.

— Then I must warn you that unless you stop this idle life, the Government may take away your child.

The smile was gone from her now. She looked at the magistrate unbelieving.

— *Dis my enigste kind,* she said, it's my only child.

— But it does not even live with you.

— There's no place, she said earnestly. The house is small.

— I am just warning you, said the magistrate. You may go.

She did not smile any more. She left the dock and followed the policeman to the door, but halfway there she halted, as though she would not go, as though something must be done or be said, as though it were unbelievable that her offences, for which she had been willing to pay without complaint, should suddenly threaten her with such a consequence. She turned and looked at me and my nephew as though she would say something to us, but she knew that she could not do such a thing in a court.

So then she went out.

— It's a lost creature, I said, that will go with any man that comes, but she has a passion for that child.

I looked at him and he was grave and tender, and nodded his head. And because he was grave and tender, and because of my love for him, I dared to say to him what I would not otherwise have dared. But I put his mother's name with it, so that if he were angry, he would not be so angry as that.

— Perhaps even as your mother and I had a passion for a child.

Then I turned away, so that if he were displeased, I should not see it. But he took my arm and led me out of the court.

— You're a foolish old woman, he said, but I get along with you.

Outside the court he left me, and I turned to watch him walk down the street, the child that had grown into such a man.

X

The roads of the grass country are full of dust on a Sunday morning, for all the people of the countryside are going to the great Church in van Onselen Street. They come in those big American cars, and cars not so big, and some by horse and trap, perhaps because they have no car, or perhaps like old Hendrik Meyer, because they have never quite felt it right to go with a car to church. You will see hundreds of cars outside the Church, and there is no dust there, because van Onselen Street was tarred to keep down the Sunday dust, and not for the comfort of Johannesburg people as some suppose. The whole white town and countryside is there, except for our few English-speaking people, and the Kaplan brothers, and those Afrikaners who belong to the Apostolics, which my brother says is no church at all; and there are even one or two Afrikaners that do not go at all, like Doctor Fouche, whether through disbelief or idleness I could not say, and him my brother would never have in our house, not even I believe if the English doctor were away and one of us was about to die. But such a habit, learned no doubt in Johannesburg and Cape Town and other godless places, is a hard habit to keep in Venterspan, for the lawyer de Villiers tried it, but now he comes like any one of us.

And there is another Sunday traffic too, that travels the big road that runs north to Johannesburg and south to Natal and Zululand. They bang the doors in the stillness, and start up their cars at the service station with a great noise of engines that can be heard in the church, and is to some a cause of anger and affront. White women get out of the cars there, laughing and smoking, wearing black glasses as though they were afraid of God's sun; and they wear trousers too, green and yellow and plum-coloured, such as no white woman should wear in a street, where all the black people watch to see what you wear and do. And I must confess, though I understand English and Jewish ways, that it is the yellow trousers that anger me most of all.

And this day I write about now was a special day in the church, because the old dominee has just got a new assistant, young Dominee Vos, and this will be his first preaching to-day. They say he can speak like an angel, but Pieter says he plays rugby football like a man possessed, with a quick shift on the leg and a dummy pass that can deceive all but the best. And if that were not enough, they say he is handsome and clever, so that my niece Martha tells me that the girls who have already seen him on the street, think that if they married a *predikant*, it would be one like Dominee Vos.

All the van Vlaanderens are there, my sister-in-law and my niece and I, but my brother is not with us, being busy with his elder's duties here and there in the church. And in front of me I can see my nephew, dressed in a dark suit, and I tell myself he is the finest looking man in all the church; and my sister-in-law looks at him too, with her look of love and care, and I know that her thought is the same as mine. And the quiet country girl Nella is there too, looking small and fair beside the big dark man. And I cannot help but smile to see that Japie is with them, and Japie is no great man for church, and got into careless ways in Pretoria; but now he will come every Sunday, because he is Social Welfare Officer now, and you could not have a Social Welfare Officer who did not go to church.

I reckon that I have heard three thousand sermons, and could have heard five thousand, except that at Buitenverwagting we had to travel far, and went to church only in the mornings. But I reckon that old Mevrou Badenhorst, who is as old as the town itself and has lived there all her life, has heard every sermon of seven thousand, maybe eight; and she still comes morning and evening, for all her ninety years, and now so deaf she cannot hear a word.

Then all the congregation stopped rustling and was still, so I turned myself to more fitting thoughts; but in any case I wanted to see what the new dominee was like.

Before the young dominee preached, old Dominee Stander said a few words about him, telling us who he was, not forgetting the rugby football. I knew my nephew would be pleased, for though the young dominee was long after his own time at Stellenbosch, they had both played in the most famous fifteen in the country. The old man told the young one that he had come to a faithful and generous people, amongst whom he himself had lived these many years, and had received every gift of loyalty and affection, which gifts he trusted the young man would deserve and be given. Which things are true, because we loved the old man, he

being a man of God, though my brother wishes he would
smoke a pipe; I do not mean he smokes cigarettes, he smokes
nothing at all.

Then the young dominee took his place, and stood there
for a moment and said not a word, looking out over the great
congregation of a thousand souls, quiet and not nervous, as
though he were the old one and we the children, but giving
no offence, because he did it quietly, and not like a man with
any vain thought in his mind. He thanked the old dominee
for his words, and gave out his text, which was about backsliders and backsliding, not those who backslid out of the
church he said, but those who backslid inside it, crucifying
the Lord anew, praising Him with their lips but denying
Him the true praise of their hearts and lives. And he invited
us to judge ourselves, because the Lord had called him to
be a shepherd not a judge, and to ask ourselves if these
things were true of us; whether we perhaps were held in
honour of men and in the market place, but within were
full of darkness. Was there a husband there who would wish
the world to know what his wife knew about him? Or perhaps his wife to know what the world, or some stranger,
knew about him? Or a son who would reveal himself to his
father, or a father to his son? Or was there any soul there
who would wish revealed to the world what he knew about
himself? He did not judge, he said; that is why he said we
were full of darkness, not deceit. For one deceit was to deceive for some base end, and the other deceit was to hide
out of fear, and for this deceit no Christian could withhold
his pity and his forgiveness, nor would God his mercy, if it
were confessed. And this mercy was beyond all computation,
abundant and healing, restoring, uplifting, and just.

No, he had not come to preach only about backsliding and backsliders, but about repentance and mercy, that a man might turn again, taking his part again in God's plan for the world, so that through a man, himself healed and refreshed, might flow a stream of living water to refresh us all, his home, his church, his town, his people, and the world.

Then all at once the young dominee stopped preaching. You could see he was a bit excited, and he slapped his hand down hard on the wood of the pulpit.

— That's the sickness of our times, he said, that we are afraid to believe it any more. We think of ourselves as men in chains, in the prison of our natures and the world, able to do nothing, but having to suffer everything. God's plan? Ah that's another thing that's done to us, history, and war, and narrow parents, and poverty, and sickness, and sickness of soul, there's nothing we can do but to suffer them.

— It's a lie, he said, and again he struck the wood with his hand. It's the lie we tell to ourselves to hide the truth of our weakness and lack of faith. Is there not a gospel of God's love, that God's love can transform us, making us creators, not sufferers? I knew a man that counted the days, each day, every day, tearing them off on the little block that stood on his desk. He was always looking at his watch, and saying, it's one o'clock or it's four o'clock or it's nine o'clock, as though it were something for satisfaction. When April went, he would say, April's gone, and wait for May to go too. I never saw him on New Year's Day, but I suppose he would have said, the Old Year's gone; he was waiting for death, though he didn't know it, because he was afraid of life, though he didn't know that either.

The young dominee's voice rose.

— I am come that ye might have life, and have it more abundantly, saith the Lord.

He closed the great book and picked up his papers and came down out of the preaching seat. The great congregation stirred and rustled, and with a kind of sigh, because this boy could preach. Then they stood up and sang, and one or two of the women wiped their eyes, which my brother never likes, because he says that religion is a matter for obedience and not for tears. I watched him too, but I did not know what he thought, nor have I ever known what passed in that mind, except those times when without warning some power stronger than his own struck him in the heart, as it did on the day when the boy did not open the parcel of the stamps. Nor did he sing in any other way than he always sang, for his obedience was constant all his days, and was not to be suddenly made greater or less by the words of any man; and indeed there were only two kinds of words that could move him at all, and they were the words of the Book and of South Africa. But the rest of us sang more deeply and loudly, because of the boy that preached.

XI

Outside the church we all met together, except my brother who had his duties, and Japie who was greeting all his friends. My nephew was holding a court, for his sister Martha clung on to his arm, and his ten-year-old nephew Koos, who was Frans's son, could not take his eyes off him. It was a private joke with us, the admiration that Koos had for his father's brother; but it was kept private, for Frans was I think a little jealous of his brother already, he himself never having been to the University, nor had he ever shone in the rugby field, nor had he ever seen a war. But it was known that Koos meant to go to Stellenbosch, and after that to be a policeman too; and his admiration was all the stranger, because he was a dark and solitary child.

My sister-in-law was happy amongst her own people, as indeed she always was. She talked to Frans and his wife and their two other children, and to Henrietta's quiet husband, who for her sake would consent to break his silent habit.

Then she touched Nella's cheek and said to her, you're looking pale.

74

The girl smiled, but she was no good at hiding, and I said to myself, there's trouble in this house. For the smile went as it came, and left her strained, and I wished she could have been cleverer at hiding.

Then my sister-in-law said, why don't you take her to the coast, Pieter?

He left his sister, and moved to the girl and took her arm, like a soldier going to duty. And she gave him a quick smile of thanks, and looked at him with love and then away, so that I knew that this trouble was no trouble of anger and words, but a thing more deep.

— Two things, he said. No leave, and no money.

— I know where you could get money, I said, from a rich woman, with no foolish pride.

He grinned at me.

— You and your money, he said.

I shook my purse at him.

— It's real money, I said. It buys and it clinks.

He smiled at his mother, but he was serious now.

— I can't go just now, he said. In any case, it'll soon be the captain's leave.

— Why don't you send her home, his mother said. For a week or two. Do it now, before Frikkie has to go to school.

— I couldn't, said Nella.

But you could see that she could, if she were spoken to enough.

— You must order her, said his mother.

He smiled at them both.

— She's got a will, he said. Like your own. It doesn't show, but it's there.

His mother said, with a smile that softened it, for a hard

thing she never had said in her life, there's only one will in our house.

— Tante has a will, said Martha.

— It's like your mother's, I said, it shows when it has to. I looked at her.

— But not so gentle, I said.

— That's what living is, she explained to us all, all wills together, and each takes a turn to yield.

Then my brother came out, and that was the end of the talk about wills. And the young dominee came out too, and we should have liked to speak with him, but there were many waiting for that; and we are a gentle family, that will wait patiently for its turn. My brother was full of jokes, and he pinched Nella's cheek too, and said she looked like a bride, which will show you that he had strange eyes; but she brightened up at his praise, and looked like a bride after all.

— You mustn't stand about on your leg, said my sister-in-law.

He growled at her.

— Shall I stand on my head, he said. Daughter-in-law, are you all coming this afternoon?

— Surely, she said.

He pinched her cheek again.

— Good, he said, I like one sensible woman in the house.

Then we said goodbye to Frans and Henrietta and their families, promising to meet them soon. I saw that my nephew was watching the young dominee, with some strange look in his eyes, and I guessed that the preaching had struck him in the heart, though I could not have told you why. Then the young dominee looked at him, and with the look in his eyes that so many young men had when they looked at Pieter van

Vlaanderen, and in a moment he was with us, with his hand outstretched, and his eyes shining

— You're Pieter van Vlaanderen, he said.

And at the sight of the boy, with his eyes shining and his face all eager, I saw what I had seen before and could not understand, that the lights went out suddenly in the house of the soul, and its doors and windows were shut and its curtains were drawn, and the man stood there outside it in the dark, with cold and formal welcome, like one who keeps you on the stoep and makes his face into the fashion of a smile, and speaks all quietly and courteous, but you know he will not ask you in.

Then he took the young dominee's hand, and bowed stiffly as some foreigners bow, and said, welcome to Venterspan.

But though I being a watcher saw these things, I was the only one. Now you cannot go to a man all shining and eager, and be bowed to stiff and cold, and not lose something of your eagerness; so the young dominee turned to my sister-in-law, and gave her a smile that would touch any woman in the world, and said, you're his mother. And with great respect he said to my brother, whom he had met already in the church, I am sorry, *meneer*, I did not realise at first who you were. But what he was saying was really other words, he was really saying, I did not realise whose father you were. And my brother looked at him out of the heavy bearded face and said nothing at all, neither with his eyes nor tongue.

Then the young dominee said to me, you're Tante Sophie, and to my niece he said, you're Martha. And we both were alive with pleasure, one like the girl she was, and one like the girl she had been. But his best smile of all he kept for Nella, as though he kept it of purpose to the last, and said to her, you're Nella. So all the women lay at his feet, and the two men stood silent and constrained.

— They called him the Lion of the North, he said to Nella. When you talk football, it's one of the things you must know. There are perhaps ten names like that, he said.

He smiled at my nephew with apology, knowing the man was constrained.

Then he said haltingly, as though he would make his praise less great, say twenty names like that.

— Tell me, he said now quite formal himself, how's the rugby here?

— It's good for a small place, said my nephew. You'll play?

At the thought of that the young dominee was formal no more, and his face was again shining and eager.

— I'll play, he said. It's . . .

He smiled at us all with that smile of his. He looked shocked at himself.

— It's almost my religion, he said.

And my brother looked at him with the heavy-lidded eyes that told nothing, and one did not know whether he cared or did not care, that it should be likened to religion to run round kicking at a ball.

The young dominee turned again to my nephew.

— You'll get your cap, he said.

My nephew shook his head.

— I'm getting old, he said.

— Nonsense. It was only the war that stopped you.

And then we said no more, because you do not speak much about the war when my brother is there, however

innocent the thing you want to say. So the young dominee
looked round, and there were still other people waiting to
speak to him.

— I must go, he said.

This time he turned to Nella first.

— Expect me soon, *mevrou,* he said.

She said to him, you'll be welcome, and thank you for
your message.

And my sister-in-law and I thanked him also for his message, and so did my nephew, though still a bit stiff. Only my
brother did not, but he bowed to the young man as you
bow to a man you recognise through a telescope; and when
the young man had gone, he walked off stiffly to the road.

And I thought to myself, how wonderful it will be at tea
this afternoon, for my nephew and his family came to us
every Sunday afternoon. And no sooner had my brother and
the young dominee gone, than Japie joined us, more like a
clown than ever.

— I didn't want to meet him, he said. He talked too much
about me in the sermon, you know, the man who watches
the clock. Especially four o'clock. That's my favourite time.

He laughed, not too loudly, but louder than another man
would laugh near a church.

— But he was wrong in one thing, he said. I don't do it
because I want to die.

*   *   *   *   *

*And I thought of what he said, that one deceit was to deceive
for some base end, and the other was to deceive from fear; and for
this deceit a man would have mercy, if it were confessed. And I
thought, I could tell this man. And I was moved to the depths*

when he said this mercy was beyond all computation, for no lesser mercy could have healed me of my sin.

But then I was appalled, knowing that I deceived, not only from fear, but for a base and ugly end; and I thought, I could not tell this man.

And then when he hit the wood with his hand, and cried out that it was a lie that we were in chains, when I saw that he believed, I said to myself again, I could speak to this man.

Then when he came to me outside the church, as a boy comes to a man, calling me the Lion of the North, I knew I could not tell him. Then he fell in love with my sister, and from her he learned to hold me even in greater honour than before. By asking me to be a diaken in the church, he silenced me for ever.

For at this time I had but one thought in my mind, and that was to tell one human soul of the misery of my life, that I was tempted by what I hated, to seize something that could bring no joy. I would have humbled myself before him, as I made the boy Dick humble himself. I would have told him every thought of my mind, I would have prayed to the Lord to give him some deep knowledge, so that he could find me a salvation, and make me clean and sweet and at peace, like my own brother Frans, like my friends, like young Vorster, like the young dominee himself.

And yet, though my need was so great, I never spoke. Was it pride that prevented me? Ah, that I do not know.

The Lion of the North! How little do men see, that a man so fresh and clean as he, should call me the Lion of the North!

Ah, was it pride that prevented me? Then to be proud, I destroyed them all!

XII

The new dominee preached again on that Sunday evening. The congregation was not so great, because few of our
farmer people came in at nights, but it was bigger than
usual, because the new dominee was to preach again. And I
was glad I came, because my nephew sat with us, Nella
having stayed with the children at home. And this time the
young dominee preached that he that asked would be given,
and he that searched would find, and to him that knocked
would be opened, out of the mercy of the Lord. But if a man
asked with half his heart he would not be given, and if he
knocked half fearing that the door would open, so that he
would go in and be thus shut off from the pleasures and comforts of the world, then it would not open. Nor if he feared
to lose the pleasures and comforts of one world, would he
find the joys of another, nor would he know the joys of any
world at all, being lost between them forever. For if God's
mercy be great, great also must be man's obedience.

And at the sound of the word obedience, my brother,
who had been grim and silent all the day, was suddenly

alive, for this was a word he understood, better than he understood the word of love. And my nephew sat there in a tight silence, and the knuckles of his hand were white through the skin, so that I knew he was moved, but I did not know why. Nor did I know till I read what he wrote. And I must tell you too that to my brother our Afrikaans language was a holy tongue, given by God in the wilderness, but never before had he heard it quite like this, for there was nothing that it could not say, nothing too deep or too strong or too quiet, so that the young man who had said to him, I did not realise who you were, meaning I did not realise whose father you were, had him nevertheless under a kind of authority.

My nephew left us soon outside the church, and walked home by himself, for he and his father were still in a constraint. The sky was clear and full of stars, and the pines gave a sound to the wind, which though it was summer was cold and fresh with the sharpness of a highveld night. It gave to the face and body a sense of cleanness and strength, restoring to a man something of youth's innocence, and a joy that one was alive.

*   *   *   *   *

When I reached my home I was calm and quiet, and I must have kissed Nella with especial tenderness, for I could see at once that she was touched.

— A fire, I said.

— I thought you'd be cold, Pieter.

She felt my hands.

— You are cold, she said.

I saw that she was solicitous for me, but nervous, and for that I was ashamed.

— Coffee, she said.

I smiled at her, and suddenly she was weeping. I took her in my arms, and she clung to me hungrily, like a child taken back into affection.

— Why are you weeping, I asked.

— Because . . .

— Yes.

— Because you smiled at me.

— I'm sorry, I whispered, I'm sorry.

— I try to love you, she said. I try every way to love you. I pray to love you more. Then . . .

— Yes, I whispered.

— You shut me out.

I held her close to me, confessing it without words. Then she drew away from me, and wiped her eyes.

— Let's have the coffee, she said.

I sat down by the fire, and she came and put the tray on the floor, and drew the small footstool against my knees, and sat on it, attending to the coffee. Then suddenly she looked up at me.

— Remember, she said.

Yes, I remembered, for so had we sat the first time I had ever touched her, in the courtship that had been so shy and simple, advancing day by day, week by week, by a word or a look, or by the accidental brushing of a hand, long enough and yet not long enough, so that it might be meant and might not be meant, so that I could lie awake afterwards and wonder, was it meant, or was it not? Our courtship was like that, long and shy and protracted; some people said it was the times, but it was not only the times, it was also our natures. I had put my hand on her shoulders, shy and my heart beating, almost as though I had made some mistake and had meant to put them somewhere else, and might take them away at any moment. Then suddenly she had put up her own, and drawn mine down to her breasts, and so astonishing was this action from one so timid and gentle, that I had buried my face in her hair, but she would have none of it, and turned up her face to my own, so that after the fashion of those times we had agreed at once to be married.

As I thought of it now I caught my breath suddenly, to think that I should have turned from that guileless boy into the grave and sombre man, not proud and self-possessed as the world took him to be, but full of unnameable desires and penitences, of resolves and defeats, not understanding himself, withdrawing and cold and silent, a creature of sorrow and evil. Why had it come about? Some people said that boys should grow up wild, and they would settle down into model husbands and fathers. Would that have been better for me?

But my upbringing could hardly have been otherwise, with a father and mother such as I had had, one strict and stern, and the other tender and loving; for one I could never openly have disobeyed, and the other I could never knowingly have hurt. My father had a code about women, as strict and stern as himself, and once I had heard him say, in a company where I was by many years the youngest, that he had never touched a woman, as a man touches a woman, other than his wife, nor had he ever desired to do so.

I remembered it well, for the company had been telling rough stories; then suddenly there was a lull, and my father suddenly said this thing, naturally and simply, as though it were a fitting part of the conversation. I felt a sudden pride, I remember, and a sudden feeling of love for him, and for his strength and certitude; and a feeling of envy too, and wonder that I was otherwise. And as he was, so was my brother Frans; but Frans was gentle and

simpler, more like my mother, and every thought he ever had could
be seen in his very face, even if he did not speak it.

Then I thought I had perhaps been too obedient as a boy, too
anxious to please and win approval, so that I learned to show out-
wardly what I was not within. Yet I was no mother's son, but
could shoot and ride with them all. I can still remember, when we
were all at the farm Vredendal, that my mother's cousin Hester
took me suddenly into her arms and said, Pieter, you come like
a wind into the house.

But perhaps when you were too obedient, and did not do
openly what others did, and were quiet in the church and hard-
working at school, then some unknown rebellion brewed in you,
doing harm to you, though how I do not understand.

— You're quiet, Pieter. What are you thinking?

And I thought, what I am thinking would frighten the wits
from your mind and the peace from your eyes, and I would tell
it if I could.

— I was thinking, I said with part of the truth, of what you told
me to remember.

And I would have liked to remind her of it, by slipping my
hands down to her breasts, but could not do it, because something
had gone wrong with it, and it would embarrass her now, here in
a lighted room. She put her head back on my knees, and I put
my hand on her cheek and throat.

— How did the new dominee preach, she asked.

— Well, I said.

— I am thinking, Pieter, she said with her eyes shut and her
voice earnest, that I need to be better, not to worry, worry, worry,
but to trust in God's providence.

And my voice caught in my throat, and I said to her, you
need to be better?

Yes, I, Pieter. When you're down, and I get down, there's no help in either of us. It grieves me to see you down.

— Does it, liefste?

— Yes. I want to help you, to get you out of the mood. But if I'm down, you think only that I'm angry, and being sorry for myself, and you hate me for it, don't you, Pieter?

I bent down and pressed my face against hers with sudden fierceness and penitence.

— I couldn't hate you, I said. Only sometimes I'm grieved for you.

— Shall we go to bed, she whispered.

I smiled at her invitation in grave agreement, for such a thing had never been a jest between us.

— Do you want to, I said.

— Yes, she whispered.

Up in the room she prayed for a long time, much longer than usual. After a while I stood up and watched her, knowing for what she prayed, for the black moods and the angers and the cold withdrawals that robbed her of the simple joys of her quiet and humble life. I said to myself, God listen to her, God listen to her, ask and it shall be given, knock and it shall be opened, search and it shall be found, before the gift and the opening and the finding are too late.

In the bed she turned on her side and pressed against me and pulled my head down to her own, and kissed me on eyes and mouth and cheeks, with a kind of fierce protection, and touched me as she knew I hungered to be touched by her, and put my hand on her breasts, and pressed the tresses of her hair against my eyes and lips, and yielded herself to me with all the childlike arts of love; and finished, curled up away from me but pressed close, and sighed with happiness and content. And I lay against her, pressing my face against her hair.

After a time I said to her, are you asleep?

— Nearly, she said.

— Why did you say, the other day, you couldn't go over it all again?

She made no answer, and I spoke quickly to reassure her, as though if I did not she might fly away.

— It was this that I meant, I said.

I raised myself up on my elbow, and looked down at her.

— You think I'm talking of physical things, I said, but I'm not. It's all together, the body and mind and soul, between a man and a woman. When you love me as you've done, I'm comforted in them all. And when I love you as I've done, it's you I love, your body and mind and soul. I'm healed, strengthened, I'll live my life as it's appointed, without the black moods and the angers.

I stopped and could not go on; but I wanted to go on, and she knew enough to know that.

— Yes, Pieter.

I knew that I was taking her again into the world that she feared, foolishly, not knowing it was the same world where she was safe and sure, not knowing that it could be yet safer and surer, but fearing it because she feared some foolish unknown that was not there at all. But it was urgent, and it must be done, and if not now and in this kind of place and at this kind of time, then never at all.

So I said to her, if you could love me more often, I'd be safe, I said.

She turned over towards me.

— Safe? Against what, Pieter?

— Against anything, my love. Against fear and danger. And the black moods.

I wanted to say, against temptation, I wanted to say, against the thing that tempts me, the thing I hate; I wanted to tell her every word, to strip myself naked before her, so that she could see the nature of the man she loved, with all his fears and torments, and be filled by it with such compassion as would heal and hold him forever.

— I pray to be made more patient and understanding, she said.

And I wanted to cry out at her that I could not put the body apart from the soul, and that the comfort of her body was more than a thing of the flesh, but was also a comfort of the soul, and why it was, I could not say, and why it should be, I could not say, but there was in it nothing that was ugly or evil, but only good. But how can one find such words?

So I said to her, I love you for that, but I ask no more than you have given me tonight.

And she was at once silent, and she was unsure, because of some idea she had, some idea that was good and true but twisted in some small place, that the love of the body, though good and true, was apart from the love of the soul, and had a place where it stayed and had to be called from, and when it was called and done then it went back to its place, and stayed till it was called again, according to some rule and custom.

— A woman has her nature, Pieter. I've told you that.

But I was silent.

— And if she goes against her nature . . . well . . .

— Well, what?

— It wouldn't be the love you want.

— I'm not talking of physical love, I said.

And she was helpless, because I was talking of that, and be-cause I was not.

I bent down and kissed her.

— I'm sorry, I said.

She put her arms round me.

— I'm stupid, she said. But I'm going to get better.

— Thank you for loving me, I said.

— I'm going to try to do better, she said. Honestly.

Then she was suddenly bright and gay, and smoothed the pillow for me, and made me lie down first, and tucked in the clothes behind my back, as you would to a child. Then she lay down too with her back to me, and nestled against me, with pleasure and content, and took my arm that was over her, and put my hand against her breast, and said, I'm happy, and in a moment was asleep.

*   *   *   *   *

Ah, had a man wanted my love, that is the love I should have given, not of any rule or custom, nor with any fear of the flesh, nor any withholding, but with the charity of love. Child, child, what thing had you done, that you should have been destroyed? For the mean and cruel were not destroyed, only the kind and gentle. And God forgive me that I should write such words, which seem to doubt His Providence, but I will be obedient even when the words seem disobedient, and will obey the voice that says to me, what thou seest, write it in a book. So child, child, what did you do to be destroyed?

*   *   *   *   *

And I suddenly thought to myself, I'll tell Kappie. I was full of excitement, wondering why I had not thought of him before. I thought of him with new affection, and with trust also, for he knew all the ways of the world, and judged them not. So I had comfort after all, and was asleep myself within the hour, which I did not think could be.

XIII

My brother's birthday parties were big affairs. We worked
for days, my sister-in-law and my niece and I, preparing the
foods, and sending the invitations by word of mouth. We invited Malan Afrikaners and Smuts Afrikaners, and the English people and the Jews, any white person indeed except
the Apostolics that my brother considered to be traitors to
the Church, and those few Afrikaners who did not go to any
church. Also we did not invite Flip van Vuuren, because although you could drink what you liked at my brother's
parties, you could not be drunk. And Flip had got very
drunk, and had gone from person to person, asking with
besotted owlishness, what's the point of living, what's the
point of life? Then in the extreme of foolishness, he went to
Jakob van Vlaanderen himself, sitting in the great chair because of the lameness of his leg, and said to him, what's the
point of living, what's the point of life? Then when my
brother had ignored him with ill-concealed impatience, he
had gone to the last extreme of foolishness, and had put his
foolish hand on my brother's arm, and my brother hating to
be touched by a stranger, and had said to him again, what's

91

the point of living, what's the point of life? So Jakob van
Vlaanderen stood up from his chair, and said in a voice of
thunder, the point of living is to serve the Lord your God,
and to uphold the honour of your church and language and
people, take him home.

So Flip's wife had to come forward, bitter and shamed,
and take him home. And my brother stood there for a full
minute, looking at us like a lion, in the silence of death,
broken only by the stumbling of the home-sent fool.

For my brother liked his liquor, and could drink more
than most, but held drunkenness and drunkards in supreme
contempt, and trousered women, and smoking women, and
the new fashion of twin beds. But he had acquired tolerance for cigarettes, though he did not smoke them himself;
and for the cinema, though he seldom went, and when he
did he would stand like a chained lion while they played
God Save the King; and he had acquired tolerance for dancing, and for Englishmen so long as they did not talk of England as home; and even in his later years for General Smuts,
reckoning that the weight of his brain had been too heavy
for his spare frame. And when his son Pieter took the red
oath and had gone to the war, he would bear no mention of
his name, but had restored him to favour when Holland fell,
not because he had any special love for Holland, but because
it was a small nation, as the Transvaal had been in 1899. This
act of restoration he had set down on paper, in language stiff
and proper, made still more stiff and proper by the language
of Holland itself, which they had taught when he was at
school. But he made it clear in his letter that this was a
change of circumstance and not of heart. And I tell you too,
so that you may know what power he had, that after it was

known about the letter, many of the young men of the grass country took the red oath and went to the war; and it is a lie to say, as some do, that a soldier could not come in uniform to our Church.

You could sit or you could stand at these parties, and you could eat heavy or light, *boerewors* and *frikkadel*, with hot meats of beef and mutton and fowl and turkey, and cold meats the same, with salads and lettuce, beetroot, tomato, cucumber, and potatoes, hot and cold, boiled and roasted, and sweetened pumpkin and squash and green peas and beans, and gravies of several kinds; and after that, *melktert* and *koeksusters* and *pannekoek* and *konfyt*. You could drink heavy or light too, orange drinks and lemon drinks, home-made not bought, and home-made gingerbeer; and all the Cape wines, the dry and the sweet, the red and the white; and the Cape brandies and the ginger and peach brandies and van der Hum; and even Scotch whisky that no one else could get at all, except perhaps the captain and the magistrate.

After my brother had said the grace, he sat down at the head of the long table because of the lameness of his leg, and those that came later would go to him to pay their respects; and he would accept them sitting, and would not stand again, except for the very old, and the captain and his mother, and the magistrate. He was gay and full of jokes, and the jokes that he liked best were the sly ones about man and wife, and the burden that each was to the other; but he drew a strict line between what was permissible and what was not permissible, yet because its exact position was known only to himself, it was best not to make such jokes at all, but just to laugh at the ones he made.

It was a family day for the van Vlaanderens. They were all there from Buitenverwagting, Frans and his wife and their children; Henrietta and her silent husband, who spoke as much at a birthday party as at any other time; Emily and her husband from Johannesburg. I myself was in and out of the room, and each time I returned to it, I looked for Pieter and Nella; and I was not the only one who was eager for them to come, for Frans's son Koos said to me, where's Uncle Pieter? Then I said he must keep watch for us both, and if I were out of the room he must come at once and call me, when his Uncle Pieter came.

So I was there when they arrived, he tall and handsome in his dark blue suit. I looked at once for his present, and I confess I was nervous when I saw it truly was a book.

— It *is* a book, I said.

— I told you it was a book.

— Pieter, what book is it?

— I told you. *The Life of Smuts.*

But when he saw I was nervous, he repented at once.

— Of course not, he said.

— What is it, Pieter?

— Wait and see, he said.

We went, he and his mother and Nella and Martha and Frans and his wife and the boy Koos and I, to the head of the long table. They put their presents on the table, and my brother pushed away his plate to deal with them the better, and I could see that he wondered what the one might be, but I am sure he did not dream it could be a book, for I told you he read no book but one; so maybe he thought it was some box or case. Nella's present was handkerchiefs, of the big coloured kind that he liked.

— Thank you, daughter, he said.

He stood up and kissed her, then sat down again. Then he opened the wrappings of the book, and could have no doubt that it would be a book. And he opened it slowly, like someone watchful. And it was a book of birds, with a coloured cover of all the kingfishers, and we all were a little more at ease, for he was a lover of all birds. But there was something else too, for the book was called *The Birds of South Africa*, and I told you that the words, *South Africa*, even in English, were holy words.

— *The Birds of South Africa*, he said in his heavy English.

He sat for a while looking at the kingfishers, with some kind of silence come over him, which kept us silent also. He opened the book, and when he saw how white and shining were the pages, he put it down again, and wiped his hands on the table napkin. Then he took out his spectacles, and took one of Nella's big coloured handkerchiefs, and wiped the spectacles, bending down over them, and taking his time, like a man taken off his guard, and wanting a moment to re-cover. Then he put on his spectacles and opened the book, and it came open at the coloured plate of the wild ducks and geese, and he studied them like a man who studied them yet did not quite study them. He turned other pages, and you could see that he was astonished that there was such a book, and by the numbers of the plates, and their colours also. His eyes went from one bird to another, and you knew that he was feeling under some kind of power of the book, and did not wish to fall under it openly; but being a clean man and honest, he did not wish to hide it altogether.

At last he said, almost like a man defeated, it's a book, it's a book. And Martha suddenly giggled and kissed him on the head, so that he growled like a lion. And my sister-in-law looked at her son with a look of pride that had all the care gone out of it, and he stood there, looking proud himself.

Then my brother growled at him, you took a risk to give me a book.

He closed it and looked at the cover again.

— An Englishman, he said, go and eat.

He pushed the book away from him, and pulled back his plate, and my sister-in-law and I took Pieter and Nella to eat, my sister-in-law holding on to her son happy and proud. Ag, but so were we all.

— You're clever, I said.

He grinned at me.

— Of course, he said. Have you just found out?

Then Japie came up, full of jokes, and he began with his Ta' Mina's and his Ta' Sophie's that I dislike, but he kissed me and that I liked. And he was pleased to see us all after all these years, but most pleased to see Pieter, and kept calling him *old brother*, which is another of the foolish expressions that he has, and he uses it, if not in every sentence, then almost as much.

My sister-in-law said to him, Japie, are you still playing rugby?

Japie's face fell at once, and from joking he was serious, because that is what rugby can do to a man.

— I haven't played for six years, he said, I'm forbidden.

My sister-in-law was at once all love and care, and said, why, Japie? And he looked downcast, indeed he cast his eyes on the floor, and said, my lungs. And my sister-in-law said gently, Japie, we hadn't heard.

He shrugged his shoulders, once, twice, and spoke as though it was a thing that had to be, and one did not weep for it any more.

— Lungs, he said. Breath. I run on the field, but my breath can't keep up with me.

Then he laughed his disgusting laugh, and all the more when he saw our faces change from concern to sheepishness.

— So I forbade it, he said.

Then he laughed again.

— The *Oubaas* will think you're drunk, I said.

We all gave a glance at my brother, but he was not attending to us, for Sybrand Wessels was sitting with him, and they were looking at the book of the birds.

— I *am* drunk, he said. Aren't I with you all again?

Ag, he could say things like that, that is why you forgave him for being a clown. We all stood and sat there, watching Pieter and Nella have their food. We had a little wine, and we laughed and remembered as though the world would go on like that forever, full of warmth and pleasure; and Japie told us many jokes, of which I write down the only one that I remember.

— Old brother, he said to Pieter, you know they sent me to Klerksdorp for a week, and I wiped out Juvenile delinquency.

Pieter humouring him, said, how?

— Well the week before I got there one *klonkie* got into trouble. But the week I was there no *klonkies* at all.

Then he laughed, in the way that by now you know. And we all laughed too. Yes, I remember that time, it was the last time we were all so together. And the light came

into the dark and sombre face, and I seeing it, and seeing
the face so changed and warm, prayed there in my heart, in
front of them all not knowing, for his peace. For though it
was Japie who talked, it was he who was the centre of us all,
he stood there tall and straight in the warmth of our love,
and it was he who destroyed us all. And why, why, why?
God knows, I do not know.

Then what should happen but that Anna should take him
away from us, right from his mother's arm; but she is a kind
of cousin, and had some kind of right, seeing we had had
him so long. She smokes and wears the yellow trousers that
I most dislike, but of course not in my brother's house, nor
in her father's either, though why she has never been found
out is a wonder to me; but she works in Pretoria and that is
maybe why. She has never married, and says openly that
Pieter is the only one she would have married, and he married someone else; and she says it so openly that one does
not know if it is true or not. She took him away from us to
get her a drink, and he turned round and grinned at us all,
and we endured it; though we were disappointed we endured it, because he turned round at us, and because we had
had him so long, and because the girl had some kind of
right. But I could have smacked her where one smacks, as I
once did when she was a child.

I saw Koos was disconsolate, and I went to him.

— Hurry, I said, there's no one with your grandfather. Go
and ask him how he likes his book.

Then I went off to the kitchen, where old Izak and Lena,
who for all their blackness were good Christian souls, were
working their heads off for the old master's party. It was a

good thing I went, for the two extra girls from the location had put all the dirty glasses in the sink, and were going to pour hot water on them. For I tell you, these great parties may look smooth and fine, but what happens in the kitchen is what counts.

XIV

Yes, I thought to myself, it's in the kitchen that the work is done. My brother must have known it, but he never thought one would be touched by a word of thanks. I felt suddenly tired and old, and pitied myself, and remembered my lip and that no man had ever wanted me. I do not dwell on these things in my thoughts, you must not think it. I count my blessings, as they say. For the Lord gave me a good home, and a little money of my own, and a brother that for all his ways was an upright man, and just; and a sister-in-law for whom I would any time die. For she gave me her children to be as my own, especially the one, and knew I loved him perhaps beyond all wisdom, and never denied me. But one does not always count one's blessings; strange it is that one should go from the sweet mood to the black in one brief moment. I went to the pantry and sat down, and stared at the floor.

— Tante, what's wrong?

I started at his voice, for I did not hear him come, but it was too late to put on another face. He came and stood by me, and lifted my rough hands, and turned them upwards and looked at them, and moved his thumbs over them with gentleness.

— What's wrong, he said.

But I would not look at him. He held my hands more tightly, but kept moving his thumbs over their roughness. Then he said, in a voice that meant he would not be silent, I asked you what was wrong.

I pulled my hands away from him.

— Ag, I said, I'm angry that I was born.

But he did not comfort or chide me, or tell me not to be a fool, or say come back to the party, or say anything at all. He stood there, not saying anything, not touching me, and I knew that I had put the black mood into him also, and for shame I could not look at him.

Then he said, it's I that should be angry I was born.

But I said to him, not looking at him, what do you mean?

But he did not answer me. I got to my feet and took him by the arms, but he looked over me, and I was not tall enough to see his eyes.

— Tell me, I said urgently, tell me.

— Ag, it's nothing, he said, it comes and it goes.

I tried to go back so that I could see his face, but he held me and would not let me, as though it were important I should not see it until he had time to recover, for he had opened the door of his soul and now repented it. And so strange was this for him, who was himself so strong and sure, and not a man for holding people unless he were in command of himself and them, that I knew it was true that he had opened the door, and that I had forced myself into it, and that he was forcing me out, so that he could shut it again. So I lost my sense, being myself tired and in the black mood, and forgot the bitter lessons that he himself had taught me in the past; and I was *vasberade*, that is I mean determined, to find out what was wrong. So I went to the pantry door and shut it, and knew the moment I had done it that I had not shut myself in but had shut myself out. He might have said to me, Tante, that's enough, or he might have said, must I teach you again, but he did not say that, seeing me standing at the door, and knowing I was already humbled and defeated.

— Tante, he said gently, I told you it comes and it goes. What about some coffee?

So I opened the door and said to him brightly, as I might have said to any man, sit down and I'll get the coffee.

Then I went and got the coffee, with only one thought in my mind, of the high wind at Buitenverwagting twenty years ago, when the boy was in the tree. For my brother and his wife and the children had gone visiting, and had left the boy, sick in bed, with me to look after him. And the servants came running to tell me the boy was in the tree. It was a cypress tree, that at the top grows frail and thin, and it was bending this way and that way in the wind, and at the top of it the boy. I called out to him to come down, but he was drunk with the power to make us afraid. I was mad with fear, and cried and screamed, as I should never have done before the black nation. Then he stretched his arms above his head, and gripped the small branches with his knees, and bent over backwards and gave some kind of cry, so that if he had fallen he would have fallen to death. I could not watch it any more, nor endure to be so shamed, and I threw my apron over my head and ran crying into the house. Then he was ashamed of his naughtiness, and afraid of what I might tell, so he came down from the tree, and went searching for me in the house, where I sat frightened and shamed and weeping.

— Tante, he said.

But I would not listen to him. He got down on his knees and pulled my hands away from my face.

— I'm sorry, tante, he said.

And at the sound of that in his voice I took him into my arms, with all the passion of a hungry woman, that would have had this child if God had given her one, and would not have asked another, and would not have asked for anything more at all, but only the time and the strength to make him into a man.

Then he stiffened in my arms and looked away from me, as though there were something of which he was ashamed. And the passion went out of me and I was afraid.

— What's the matter, I said.

— I don't like it, he said.

— What?

— To be kissed like that.

Then he went away and got into his bed, and that was the way of it. And from that day he had the power over me. And because of that day I did not speak when I should have spoken, and because of me he was destroyed.

* * * * *

When I went back to the pantry with the two cups of coffee, Japie was there, come in search of his friend. He was calling him old brother in every second thing that he said, and opening all the tins in the pantry, as though there were not food enough in the big room where my brother's party was.

— Coffee, Ta' Sophie, he said. You're a wonder.

— The one cup's for Pieter, I said, and the other's for me. And if you want coffee you'll find it in the big room. And don't Ta' Sophie me. And put back the lid on that tin.

Japie turned to my nephew and said to him, ask her for another cup of coffee, she'll do it for you.

And the dark face lit up, with that lamp that I told you of, that is the lamp of the soul.

— Ag, I said, I'll get the coffee.

When I came back again, Japie said to me, what about the girl Stephanie?

— What about her, I said.

— Must I take her child away?

I sat and considered it.

— You must wait, I said. You must wait till she comes out and give her a chance to work.

— What d'you think, old brother?

— That's what I think, said my nephew. But you're the expert. What do *you* think?

And when he heard that he was an expert, Japie was at once like a judge, what the English call *pompous*, not that I mean for a moment that judges are pompous, but I mean it is pompous to be like a judge when you are not a judge, and what I mean is that sometimes one language has the word, and sometimes the other.

— I'd ask one question, said Japie; is she fond of the child?

And my nephew and I said together, yes, she's fond of the child.

— That's important for a child, said Japie in a manner a bit grand. We begin to think. . . .

And here he looked about him, and you could see he was a bit sorry to be talking in a pantry.

— We begin to think, he said, that lack of affection is one of the greatest causes of juvenile delinquency in a child, even if it is . . . well . . . illegitimate. . . .

And he gave me a little bow.

— I regret, Tante Sophie. . . .

— Don't be a fool, I said, I knew about it before you were born.

— Assuming then, he said a bit stiffly, that you take an illegitimate child from its mother, and give it some kind of legitimacy, but that affection is lacking in the new inter-personal . . .

— Do you know what my brother calls those, I said.

— No.

— He calls them the university words.

And though Japie was hurt, the dark face lit up again, so that I was glad to have thought of such a clever thing.

— So we'll give her the chance, I said.

And Japie nodded, a bit too angry to say any more words.

— *Hemel*, I said (and I do not often use such words), we must go.

For my brother's parties stop sharp at half-past ten, and it was almost that time.

After they had all gone, the family stayed behind, Pieter and Nella, and Frans and his wife, and Henrietta and Emily and their husbands, and of course those of us in the house. And I brought my brother the Book, the great one that came

from the Cape in 1836, and has all our van Vlaanderen
names. And my brother knows the Book from the first word
to the last, and always turns to it just where he wishes. It
was his custom, on the occasion of any event, to turn to some
special place, and if he had a genius, it was a genius for finding the words. But this night I saw that he pondered it,
while we all sat silent. And he turned to one place, and read
it to himself, and rejected it; and what it was, I should have
liked to know, because it might have given some deep meaning to this book. But he rejected it.

Then he read.

*   *   *   *   *

*Then Job answered the Lord, and said, I know that thou canst
do everything, and that no thought can be witholden from thee.
Who is he that hidest counsel without knowledge? Therefore have
I uttered what I understood not; things too wonderful for me,
which I know not. Hear, I beseech thee, and I will speak; I will
demand of thee, and declare thou unto me. I have heard of thee by
the hearing of the ear; but now mine eye seeth thee. Wherefore I
abhor myself, and repent in dust and ashes.*

*   *   *   *   *

And then he was silent, as though he considered it, and
my sister-in-law watching him with the eyes of love, and all
of us silent, and I, at least, daring to wonder whether this
could truly be, that he read such a thing because his son had
given him a book of coloured birds.

Then he read again, starting at the eleventh verse.

*   *   *   *   *

Then came there unto him all his brethren, and all his sisters, and all they that had been of his acquaintance before, and did eat bread with him in his house; and they bemoaned him, and comforted him over all the evil that the Lord had brought upon him; every man also gave him a piece of money, and every one an earring of gold. So the Lord blessed the latter end of Job more than his beginning.

*   *   *   *   *

Then my brother prayed, but made no more mention of these things. And Pieter and Nella left last, and my sister-in-law and my niece and I saw them to the door, and the mother pulled down the son's head and whispered something to him. And what words she said to him I do not know, and I never asked her what they were, but I write down here that she said, this was one of the days of my life. And I saw that the dark face looked at her, not alight as it sometimes could be, but with some look of love and grief.

XV

I suppose it was the success of the birthday party that made that time so happy that I still remember it. But in any case it is the time of year that I love the best, when the summer turns slowly to winter. Mind you, I like the world when it is green, and I like it when it is yellow; but I like it best of all when it begins to turn, and the dew lies thick upon the bushes, and you leave your footsteps on the lawns. And perhaps I liked it best because my life was turning also, and the angers and moods of the heats of summer came less often, and the mind was filled, like the veld itself, with some promise of rest and peace. And the early mornings were beyond my wit to tell about, full of coolness and freshness, and the whole world wet and sparkling with the dew. And I tell you too, hoping you do not weary of me, that in all those days of coolness and the turning of the leaves, and of my duties in the house and in the town, and of my work with our Women's Welfare Society, and of the joy that I had of my gentle sister-in-law and her love, that my greatest joy of all, all day and every day, was in the tall dark man who had my name.

And we saw him more often too, because Nella and the children went away, down to her father and mother on the farm Vergelegen, which means Placed Far, and placed far it was, being on the very edge of the grass country, where it falls to the world of rock and thorn and the hot red flowers, near the great Park where the lions are.

Her father came for her, and he was a tall fierce old man, with a face like an eagle, and the bluest and most piercing eyes that I have ever seen. They came to my brother's house to say goodbye, but for all his piercing eyes he did not recognise me, but took me for my sister-in-law, although I wear no rings at all. He asked me how were my other children, and my brother snorted like a bull, and blew hard at his nose.

I said sharply, you had better ask my sister-in-law, she has some children.

And my brother snorted still louder, and blew still harder at his nose. For he always said of Nella's father that you could put his sense of humour into a match-box already full.

Then it was time for them to go, and I could see that the girl was sad and yet glad to go, and I know now that she knew that something was going wrong, and thought perhaps that rest and separation would cure it. And the lieutenant let her go willingly and unwillingly, for she had been more loving to him, and had done what she said she would do, prayed and tried to be more understanding. And he took her small gifts, as one takes the gifts of a child, as a man in a deep money trouble takes the pence of some poor friend, never dreaming to tell him it is not enough.

At this time of the turning of the year it was all rugby football in Venterspan and Sonop and Bremerspan and Rus-

fontein. You could see all the boys, every afternoon in the
street, in their shorts and coloured jerseys, and the heavy
boots that made such a noise in a house. And when night fell
every place where they lived was full of the sound of running water and cries for soap, and they came out of their
baths and showers with red and shining faces, looking full
of health and clean and strong, so that we felt proud that
they were our boys. And by that I mean the English as well,
though it is true that it is the Afrikaners who are really the
rugby nation.

I went down myself to see them practice on the field
which old Koos Slabbert gave them from his farm; and you
could see his windows shut, because his wife disapproved of
the coarse rugby language, and disapproved of rugby too,
because somewhere, some other place, some boy was killed.
And I went there to give myself the secret pleasure of watching the tall dark man, and of seeing him in authority, and of
seeing the others come to him, and speaking to him as boys
speak to a master at the school. He stood apart with pieces
of paper with all their names, and he and Hannes de Jongh
would talk about them; and now the young dominee was
always standing with them too, because these three were the
best players of them all. Then they would play, but I would
not see him as much as I wished, for he was always down in
the scrum; but sometimes he would get up, like Samson of
the Book, and shake them off like water, and lift his hands
above them all, and send the ball sailing across the field for
others to catch and run. I would get excited and tell myself
not to be a fool, because a practice is only a practice, and
one does not laugh and clap as one does in a match, for then

you can laugh and clap as much as you please, being one of thousands, and not just a foolish woman proud of a man.

And Japie was the referee, though how he could referee so far from the ball I could never see. I remembered his joke that when he ran his breath couldn't keep up with him, but it would have been true to say that he stayed behind with his breath. Sometimes he would stop near me and put his hand to his side, looking at me with a great look of anguish and pain, like a man who was about to die, but would joke to the last.

He was once so far behind the ball that he blew the whistle for something that had not happened at all, and the young dominee protested. But Japie in spite of his suffering gave him a proud and haughty look, and said, *never argue with the referee.* For on the field even a dominee is below the referee.

And the dominee would sometimes get the ball, and go weaving in and out, with his hair flying behind him and smiling like an imp, like no dominee I have ever seen, with Bible and Church all forgotten, at least that was how it seemed, though I do not think it was really so. And Martha used to come with me too, and I told you I am a watcher, and no fresh girl can hide from me, but of course I said never a word.

And after the game some would go to the Royal for a drink of beer, and then you could hear the laughing and shouting from the bar, the kind of thing some women fear; but I have never feared it, for rugby itself is coarse and rough, and my own brother, who never touched but one woman in his life, can be coarse and rough himself. And it is a strange thing that his son never jested coarse and rough, and no one jested with him coarse and rough; and whether that was because of his mother, or because of some deep thing that twisted wrong, God knows, I do not know.

*   *   *   *   *

That is something I do not understand. I never made such a joke, not even to myself. When I sat in the bar they would never make such jokes to me, sometimes even they would fall silent when I came in. I remember when they wanted Sakkie to tell the joke about the boomslang, and Sakkie smiled at me and said, I'll tell you when Pieter's gone. Yet they were all cleaner and sweeter than I. That is a thing I never understood.

*   *   *   *   *

It was after one of these practices that he came to the house for dinner, his dark face red and clean from the rugby and the bath.

And he said suddenly to his father, father, you don't look well.

And my brother, who had been trifling with his food, growled at him, why am I not well?

— I think you don't look well.

And my brother, who had not looked at him yet, went on playing with his food, and growled again, ah, so you're a doctor now.

— I tell him it's the influenza, said my sister-in-law, with her smile of love and care.

— Of course it's the influenza, I said.

— Women, said my brother. They like a man to be sick so they can put him in a bed, then they can master him.

— It's a day in bed he needs, said my sister-in-law.

— I never spent a day in bed in my life, he said. I'm too old to start now.

— You were six weeks in bed with your leg, I said.

— Sickness, he said irritably. I'm talking of sickness.

And I went back through my memory, knowing that there was such a day. Then I remembered it.

— Who had to get out of his bed to see his second daughter when she was born?

That was my niece Emily, who came after Pieter and Frans and Henrietta. And she was called after Emily Hobhouse, who came out from England to work for our people during the English War. As soon as I mentioned it, I could see that I was under his guard, and had he been a man less proud he would have smiled; but he did not smile, he suddenly wrinkled up his nose and scratched it, which I think he always did to draw together the muscles of his face so that it would not smile. Then when he was recovered he turned and looked at me, and his eyes went up and down my face, as though it were some strange creature that he saw.

— Tante Sophie must write a history of the van Vlaanderens, he said to his son. All the dates will be right, and all the facts be wrong.

Then he was of a sudden animated.

— I said sickness, he said. And that day I wasn't sick. I was worried about my wife.

— It was her fourth child, I said.

— A good husband, he said, is worried even at the twentieth child. And Sophie, your memory is so good, do you remember what old Doctor Harper said to me?

— No, I said.

— When he saw me lying in the bed, he said to me, Mr. van Vlaanderen, saying my name as an Englishman does, I've brought hundreds of children into the world, and never lost a father yet.

We all laughed, and I waited till we had finished laughing.

— It's a good story, I said, but Doctor Harper was dead. He glared at me.

— Who was it then?

— Dr. Matheson.

He snorted.

— An Englishman, he said. That's good enough, it was an Englishman.

— He wasn't an Englishman, I said. He was a Scot.

— In God's name, he said . . .

And then he stopped, for he is ashamed to use God's name, and I was sorry to have made him do it.

— There's a devil in you tonight, he said.

Then he signed to me for the Book, and when the prayers were over, I said to him, now if you're sensible you'll go to bed.

— You and your bed, he said irritably.

— That's what your cousin Abraham said, and went out working in the fields in the rain. And left you that poor creature of a wife and that great family to look after. His boasting cost you a penny.

He chuckled.

— Abraham, he said. You remember the year of the big wind, how he couldn't get home and had to go into the wattle plantation, and come back tree by tree? But you're right. It cost me a penny.

His strange wit came into him, and he looked at his son.

— That's why Pieter had to go to Stellenbosch, he said, because I couldn't afford Oxford and Cambridge, and all that rowing in the boats.

He rose heavily.

— But I'll please you, he said. I'll go to bed now, and Sophie, you'll make me a brandy with boiling water, and half a teaspoon of sugar, and a piece of lemon. . . .

— There are no lemons, I said.

He took a step or two, then without turning called to his son; and for some reason I cannot give, that was a habit of his, to start to leave a room, and then to stop, and to talk with his back turned.

— Pieter, have you ever seen the phalarope?

— The what, father?

— The phalarope.

My brother added impatiently, a bird.

Then his son, for politeness sake, took a step or two also until he stood by his father, but his father still did not turn to him, but stood as he was before.

— No, father.

— That Englishman of yours says they're birds of the coasts. Have you ever seen the *ruitertjie*, at the farm at Buitenverwagting?

— Yes, father.

— And you've seen the phalarope there too, but you always thought it was the *ruitertjie*.

— It could be, said his son doubtfully.

His father turned to him.

— I didn't say it could be, he said, I said it was. Do you think I was blind when I was young?

— No, father, but . . .

But his father had turned round and faced us all. It gave him pleasure that we were all listening to him, but I write down here that it was not a vain pleasure, it was more a kind of mischief.

— I have two good eyes, as good as any youngster's of today. And when I am recovered from this dangerous illness that so grieves you all . . .

And here he bowed to us a little.

— . . . then I'll show you a phalarope, he said.

He turned again to his son.

— It's not the only mistake in that book. Goodnight, son. Goodnight, Sophie; Martha, are you taking me up the stairs, seeing I am so weak?

The girl was up and took him by the arm. But at the foot of the stairs my brother stopped and turned the girl about to face us, and I knew something was coming.

— She's a good girl, he said. She's always at the church.

Ah, I told you he had strange eyes, that could see so much and so little. Martha blushed and he turned her about at once, and she took him up the stairs. And her mother smiled to herself, her smile of care and love, while I looked at my nephew, who looked at first surprised, and then the small furrow came between his eyes, as though he had suddenly remembered something with pain.

But I tell you the story of this night, because it was part of the happy time that I remember, just when the summer was turning into winter, when the days are fresh and clear, and the sun is shining from the morning till the night. And the rain goes, and the whole world lies in sun from April to September; and the cosmos come out along the roads and in the fields, great sheets of white and pink and red, and the golden leonotis too, whose flowers children pick and suck for the sweet and sickly juice. And sometimes it happens, once in a spell of years, in some month when no rain should be, that the great clouds come up, banking and black, with the thunder and lightning of some steaming summer, and pour down their water on the earth, sweeping away roads and bridges, and drowning people at the drifts. So did my summer turn, not into quietness and peace, but to the dark black storm that swept us all away.

Ah, but I did not mean to tell you that. But then perhaps I did, for I had the warning on that night. Yet it was really in my mind to show you my brother in his house; for some said he was a hard and loveless man, and would ride down any that stood in his way, without pity or mercy. But I tell you it was not true.

Then I went to the kitchen and when I came back I said to my nephew, old Isak wants to see you.

— I'll go, he said.

And I heard great talking there in the kitchen while I was in the pantry. It reminded me of the days in the kitchen on the farm Buitenverwagting, when he was a boy. Isak and Lena were asking after Nella and the children and they still called him *kleinbasie*, which is small master, though it is a strange name now for so tall a man.

* * * * *

Old Isak said to me, there's a woman asking to see you, and I told him to bring her in. And it was the girl Stephanie. She stood there smiling and frowning, and would look up and look down, and played with her hands. And I asked her what she wanted.

— I've come to tell the baas, she said, I'm working.

— Where, Stephanie?

— For Baas Willemse, she said.

— That's good, I said.

And I said to her, why do you come to tell me?

Her smiling and her frowning went at once, and she stopped playing with her hands.

She said to me earnestly, so that the baas can tell the Government.

— That's Baas Grobler's work, I said.

But she said, sweeping it aside, I came to the baas.

And I said, why?

At that moment I was alone there with the girl, and she said to me in a low voice, because the baas would do it for me.

And the mad sickness came over me, that God knows I do not want, that God knows I fear and hate. And I did not say to her in a voice of every day, do not be foolish. I did not even say to her, how can you know such a thing? I said to her, quiet and trembling, how did you know? And she raised her head and smiled, not quite submissive nor quite bold. Then in an instant the smile was gone, and she said to me, not any longer with that fierceness with which once she said it, but servile and whining, it's my only child, it's my only child. Therefore I knew that someone else was there; and I was angry and afraid too, not so much because of the boldness of the look, as of the poor pretence that followed it. So I did not turn, but I said to her warningly, and what about the liquor?

— I shall never be caught again, she said.

— You thought that before.

— The baas does not understand, she said. I will never make it again.

— And the child?

— It is with me here, in the location.

— Good, I said. And listen . . .

— Yes, baas.

— I shall tell Baas Grobler that you are working.

She thanked me and went out, and then only did I turn and look at my aunt Sophie. But she did not look at me.

*   *   *   *   *

No, I did not look at him. How could I look at him? For now suddenly, and it unwanted, I had found what I had searched for all these years, and it was more dark and terrible than anything I had feared. The heart was stopped in me, and I could not look at him at all. And I prayed to the Lord God on my knees, half an hour, an hour maybe. And I prayed in my bed, and could not sleep for what I thought and prayed. Then I slept, and woke when the clock struck three, and reproached myself that I had made so much of the bold look of a girl; and having reproached, I prayed again. Though the night was cold I got out and prayed on my knees, as though I might better reach the ears of God in Heaven. When I slept again I do not know, but the birds were twittering in the trees. And when I woke again, I prayed again, and thought I was a fool, for thinking the unthinkable. For what had I seen but an idle girl look boldly at a man? And had I not heard him say, in the voice of his authority, what about the liquor? And had the girl not changed, from boldness to whining, just because she knew that I was in the Welfare Society, that threatened to take her child? So I comforted myself, with the thought that my love had made me mad. Yet I was not really comforted, because I am a watcher, and knew that no such girl might look in such a way at such a man. So I went from comfort to fear the whole day long, knowing and not knowing, and if I knew, not knowing what to do. Yet what made me most to fear was not what I had seen, but because I remembered he had said, I am angry that I was born.

XVI

So the girl Stephanie went to work for Coenraad Willemse. She came from the location at six in the morning and went back to it at eight of night, and he paid her forty shillings a month, which is less than you get for breaking the law and making beer. And some woman said to Mevrou Willemse, I hear you have Stephanie now, and this woman laughed, and made Mevrou Willemse feel a fool and simple. For white and black live in separate worlds, and how many would know about the girl Stephanie, and her breakings of the law and her goings to prison? And how many would know about her nameless child? Indeed I should not have known myself if we had not started the Women's Welfare Society.

So Mevrou Willemse told her husband of the woman who had laughed because of the girl Stephanie and he, not wishing to be more of a fool, went privately to some friend who knew about such things, and asked him who was the girl Stephanie, and his friend told him about the liquor and the prison and the child. And the Willemses were angry that they had to lose the girl, for she worked like a slave for her forty shillings, and she was better than any girl they had had before; for the Willemses had a new servant every few weeks, not like ourselves, who have had Isak and Lena all their lives, because my brother is just and his wife gentle. But Mevrou Willemse had a tongue that was sharp and cruel, and she would follow a girl all over the house, from room to room, and nag at her with spite for some trifling thing; and she would make her pay from her forty shillings for some broken cup, and never show her any sign of love.

And the Willemses were angry with the girl too, that she should come into their holy home, and bring with her such deceit and sin. But most of all they were angry because some silly woman laughed. Therefore they put her on the street, and paid her only for the days that she had worked, which is against the law; but it is a safe thing to do in Venterspan, where the black people are humble and obedient, and do not know the tricks of justice.

And that night my nephew was busy with his stamps, and the black boy Johannes that worked in the kitchen had gone to bed, when there came the knock on the kitchen door. And he opened it, and there was the girl Stephanie. And the whole town was still and dark, but for the sound that the wind makes in the trees.

*   *   *   *   *

So I said to her, and my voice was trembling; what do you want? And she looked about her, and then she suddenly came past me into the kitchen. And I shut the door.

— Baas, she said.

— Yes.

— Baas, I have lost the work:

— Why?

— They sent me away.

— Why?

— They found out. About the prison. And the child.

And I said to her desperately, why do you not go to Baas Grobler?

— I came to the Baas, she said.

Then she smiled at me, and the mad sickness that I hate and fear came over me, and she knew it, it being one of the things that she understands. I should have said to her, this is not my work. I should have said to her, go to Baas Grobler again. I should have said to her, let them take your child, and send you to prison, let them throw you into the street, let them hang you by the neck until you are dead, but do not come to my home, nor smile at me, nor think there can be anything between you and me. For this law is the greatest and holiest of all the laws, and if you break it and are discovered, for you it is nothing but another breaking of the law. But if I break it and am discovered, the whole world will be broken.

— Then she said to me, where are the mistress and the children?

And I, knowing that she knew, said unwillingly, they're away.

— That's a pity, she said.

Then suddenly I said to her, wait.

I went up to my room, and there in the pocket of my uniform I found two notes and some silver. And I looked at the beds in the room, Nella's and mine, and the two small beds for my children. And I knelt down at my bed, and I said, o God wees my genadig, o Jesus Christus wees my genadig. Then I came down with the notes and the silver.

— Take this, I said, so that you will not need to make more liquor. And go again and look for a job.

— I'll go tomorrow, she said.

She put out her two hands to take the money and was full of thanks.

— I'll go to every house in the town, she said. And when I have a job I'll let the baas know.

And I said to her in a low voice, do not come any more to this house.

But I did not say it as I should have said it. I must have said it differently, though God be my witness I did not mean it. For she said to me, when I am working, I go home at eight o'clock, past the place where the baas saw me running.

I made no answer to that, but stood half away from her, looking at the stove. And when she saw that I made no answer, she said, goodnight Baas. And I said, Goodnight Stephanie. And she opened the door quietly and was gone.

Then I went back to the stamps but I could not put my mind to them. For God forgive me, my mind was on the girl, half with madness, and half with apprehension that she could think she could come to my house. And a great longing came over me for Nella and the children, and for their love and for the noise in the house, and for the touch of them, and for their safety. Perhaps I could have told her that night that I had been tempted and resisted; yet perhaps I could not. How I wondered at myself, that I who shrank from any dirty joke, and was so fussy about my body and clothes, especially my shirts and handkerchiefs, should be tempted by such a thing, for I notice always a man's and woman's nails, and I shudder when a man clears his throat and spits, and pulls a dirty handkerchief from his pocket. I could never sleep on a soiled pillow, and it was painful to me to go into one of the lavatories that they seem to have in every garage and service station that I ever saw, full of oil and muck and papers. I have annoyed Nella more than once, by asking for a clean tablecloth when the coffee or the beetroot had been spilled on the old. She might argue about the coffee, and I give in; but never about the beetroot, knowing that I would rather take my food to the study and eat there alone. If I stayed in a hotel, I was always constrained like any country boy, and would take patiently just what they would do or not do, or give or not give, and walk about delicately as even the waiters had more right than I. I remember yet in Johannesburg, when they gave me the dirty tablecloth that I sat there with the anger climbing up my throat, till I could endure it no longer, and I stood up and said in a cold and toneless voice, must I sit here with this filth? Then when they saw my great height, suddenly I who walked there delicately was treated like a king and feared, and they rushed about me and put things right that I had not noticed at all, and something of my father came into me and I laughed at them in my heart, and something of my mother came into me, and I was ashamed.

As I sat there my mind went back suddenly, ten, no eleven years, to Stellenbosch. I could see the very room where we were sitting, five or six of us students. Moffie de Bruyn's room with the old Vierkleur on the wall and the picture of President Kruger. We were talking of South Africa, as we always talked when it was not football or psychology or religion. We were talking of colour and race, and whether such feelings were born in us or made; and Moffie told us the story of the accident in Cape Town, how the car crashed into the telephone box, and how he had gone rushing to help, and just when he got there the door of the car opened and a woman fell backwards into his arms. It nearly knocked him over, but he was able to hold her, and let her gently to the ground. And all the time the light was going off and on in the telephone box. And just when the light went on, he saw it was a Malay woman that he had in his arms, full of jewels and rings and blood. And he could not hold her any more; he let her go in horror, not even gently, he said, and even though a crowd was there. And without a word he pushed through the crowd and went on his way. For the touch of such a person was abhorrent to him, he said, and he did not think it was learned; he thought it was deep down in him, a part of his very nature. And many Afrikaners are the same.

Why Moffie's story should come back to me then I do not know, for I cannot remember that I had ever thought of it all these eleven years. But it came back to me now, and I thought of him, and of all those like him, with a deep envy, and a longing too, that I could have been like that myself.

How we laughed at Moffie's story, partly because of the way he told it, and partly, I suppose, because we were laughing at ourselves. I do not think we were laughing at the Malay woman, nor at the way he let her fall to the ground. And I suppose there was some shame in it too. But I would take the shame, and I would be like that myself, if I could; for to have such a horror is to be safe. Therefore I envied him.

*   *   *   *   *

Then suddenly he decided to go to Kappie and to tell him these strange things, knowing that Kappie understood the ways of the world and did not judge. And suddenly it seemed easy to him, for these were human things, and they happened in men, and one should be able to talk about them. And they would talk about them, without horror or judgment, quietly and smoking, and it would be easy to say to Kappie, you know, Kappie, I am like that myself. And it troubles me, so that I am full of black angers and moods, and that is why I hold back within myself, and men are afraid of me, and will not tell me a story in a bar. And Kappie, what do I do? In God's name, what do I do?

When he reached the store, he was nervous and constrained. He went to the room at the back, where Kappie lived alone, with his stamps and his great stinkwood cabinet full of all the records of all the music in the world, and the small stove with the kettle and the cups, and the small bird that was his friend and sang to him all the day. He was nervous because he had never been at such an hour before. And you cannot say to a man, I am come to talk to you of this and that, and when we are ready, I shall tell you of the deep misery of my life, and you must help me, you must help me in God's name, before I am destroyed, and you must find some magic for me, you must tell me something in God's name, you must make some plan for me because I have never told such things to a man before. You must make some rule, that I can follow, something known only to you and me, and I will obey, you need not worry that I shall not obey, only to be safe, to have a rule before I am destroyed, for God's mercy's sake.

He knocked at the door, and Kappie opened it to him. And when he saw the lieutenant he was full of pleasure, and asked him in, and put him into his own chair.

— Kappie, I'm sick of the empty house, and I'm wanting to see some stamps.

And Kappie told me that his lips trembled when he said, I'm wanting to see some stamps, so that Kappie knew that he wanted something deeper than any stamps. So they looked at Kappie's South African stamps, of the old Cape of Good

Hope and Natal and the old Republics, and strange stamps that they used in the waggon days, and stamps of the republics of Stellaland and Goshen that are now forgotten, and stamps where something was left out or something put in or something printed upside down or sideways, and the greater the foolishness the more you pay for the stamp. Then they made coffee on the stove, and Kappie played the Tchaikowsky Concerto, that is to me one of the greatest pieces of music that any human soul has ever imagined, and where such sounds come from, and how they come into the mind of a man that once was a child sucking at a nipple with sobs and tears, God knows, I do not know. And Kappie put out the light, as he always does for such music, and they sat there with only the glow from the stove, and he watched the lieutenant, not staring at him at all, but watching as I watch, with no one knowing. And he told me that the Concerto was great music, but no greater than the trouble of the lieutenant's soul, that they matched each other there in the dark so that the music sounded to him as it had never sounded before, with new deepness and sorrow.

And when the Concerto was finished, the lieutenant stood up and said, Kappie, I must go home.

— You'll come again, lieutenant?

— Yes, Kappie, I'll come again. I've enjoyed it.

Then Kappie said, you can come every night if you wish. What could be better, stamps and coffee and music and your company?

And the lieutenant could not answer him, and Kappie did not put on the light, and they went to the door, and the lieutenant said to him, not looking at him, Goodnight, Kappie, in a strange voice not his own, and he said none of the things that men or women say when they part, about the beauty or coldness of the night, or the first frost that has already come to the high parts of the grass country. He said nothing at all, but went without another word, and it was a strange ending to an evening already strange.

And Kappie went back to his room and shut the door, and stood at the door. Then he walked a pace or two, and stood again. Then he walked again to his chair, and sat down on the edge of it, looking at the floor. But he could think only of two things, and one was Nella, and the other was money trouble. But something told him that it was neither, but some tragic trouble of the soul; and the Jews understand about the soul.

Ah, if he could have told. For where would he have found a man more true and faithful? And where would he have found a man who would better have understood and would not have shrunk from him? And yet he could not tell.

And as I write here I read it again, the very paper is in front of me—

*　　*　　*　　*　　*

But I would take the shame, and I would be like that myself, if I could; for to have such a horror is to be safe. Therefore I envied him.

*　　*　　*　　*　　*

I have met Moffie de Bruyn myself and he was as ordinary a man as one could meet, and full of vanity. So when I read that he envied him, I could not see to read at all.

XVII

Well, my brother went to bed after all. For two or three days he resisted it, grumbling and growling, and picking at his food. Then he went to bed, complaining that he had been forced by nagging women, and would go if only to escape. The English doctor came, and it was influenza true enough; but the doctor said to me privately that he didn't like the sound of my brother's heart, and as my duty was, I told my sister. So we spent much time in my brother's room. But I tell you he enjoyed himself when the worst of the influenza was over. Dominee Stander came to see him and the captain, and Sybrand Wessels. With the dominee he talked church matters, solemn and serious, and with the captain he talked grave and austere, each smoking his pipe. But with Sybrand Wessels he talked everything, politics and farming and Russia. Then they would have a drink of brandy (which he otherwise never touched in the day) and then would start the sly jokes, a bit coarse and rough; you could hear them chuckling over them, but if either of us came up, or his daughter Martha, you could hear them shushing each other like a pair of girls. And when we came in Sybrand would say, *Ja, nee,* as though he could not let the joke go

entirely, and he would snort and giggle like an old fool. My
brother would watch him with a kind of devil in him, because there was no brandy in the world that could make
him foolish, but I tell you that only Sybrand would have
been allowed to do such a thing. And they laughed most
over the coarse story of Bram Boshof's little house which
was one of those places that you find on a farm, built over
a pit; and Bram's brother-in-law Hennie, whom he did not
like, came to the farm to spend Christmas. And when Hennie
went to the little house, Bram set off one of those Christmas
fireworks under him in the pit. Then Hennie came rushing
out, not even decent, and Bram rushed to meet him, shouting, My God, you're a low man, to make such a noise in my
little house. So Hennie packed his bags and went off in a
great anger, with Bram's wife all weeping, and Bram both
ashamed and pleased.

Then my brother lay back in the bed and watched old
Sybrand, for my sister-in-law and I had just come in, and
Sybrand had had some brandy, and Sybrand pulled himself
together, but my brother would look at him to remind him,
and Sybrand would snort, and then blow his nose, and be
in a great distress, whilst my brother watched him with the
devil in his eyes.

Then they would get out the book of the birds, and go
through it all again, sometimes pleased with the Englishman
that made it and sometimes pitying him for his lack of
knowledge. When Sybrand was gone my brother would
read the Bible, not the great Bible that would have been too
heavy for him, but a smaller one; then the coarse jokes
would be forgotten and he would read and ponder in the
Book.

And I remember the night that his son came, and after prayers we all sat in the room, except Martha, who was gone to something at the church. My brother was not so well that night, and did not even smoke his pipe. He said very little, but we three sat and talked, and we made the coffee over the fire in his room, which is a thing he likes.

After the coffee he looked at his son out of the heavy eyes, made heavier by the influenza.

— When do you get a holiday, he asked.

— When the captain . . .

— I don't mean the long holiday, he said irritably. I mean a day.

— I might get off on Empire Day.

My brother grunted, for he hated the name of Empire Day; and he hated it doubly too, because it was also the birthday of General Smuts.

— You mean the twenty-fourth of May, he said.

— Is there anything you want, father?

My brother said very slowly, almost grudgingly, because he himself would have taken more time to reach such a point, I thought we might go for a day to Buitenverwagting.

And the dark face lit up at the thought of going to Buitenverwagting.

— We could have a picnic, I said.

— If you are asked, my brother said.

Now though my brother often said such things, and though the sharpness of his tongue was not always meant to hurt, yet he knew that my face fell; for he growled at once, yes, we could have a picnic.

Then he said firmly, not at the pan. In the Long Kloof if you like.

— Why not the pan, I said.

— Pieter and I are going to the pan, he said.

I looked at my sister-in-law and saw that she was not looking at us at all, but at her hands quiet in her lap, and I knew what she was knowing, that she was listening to unusual words such as she had never thought to hear spoken, but which she had prayed to hear these many years. But I knew also that my brother knew what was in our thoughts, and that the thing that he had tried to say carelessly and naturally was crying itself out aloud in the room. He closed his eyes as though he were tired, and made a movement as though he had felt some sudden pain through lying so long in bed.

— Can you take the car to the pan, he asked.

— Easily, father.

Then my brother opened his eyes, and they were suddenly alive and mischievous.

— We'll take the glasses and the book, he said, and see if we can find the phalarope.

— The phalarope?

— But it's no use going on your Empire Day. You see, this phalarope isn't an English bird, and it won't wait for Empire Day. It'll be gone by then, to Russia or some other place.

— I could take a day before then, father.

— Good.

He turned to his wife and me.

— This phalarope that no one has ever seen, is clearly a very shy bird, he said. That's why I want no women and children nagging and screaming around the pan.

He was quiet for a moment.

— I'll teach an Englishman, he said, to write about our birds.

Then he was jovial and teased my sister-in-law and me, though about what things I cannot now remember. And his son sat silent, not sombre, but quiet and grave. And when I looked at him, with the cleanness of the rugby shining out of his eyes and face, I felt a fool for my fears, and for tormenting my soul with the bold look of an idle girl. And I tried to remember if he were looking at her when she gave him the bold look, because if he were not, it could be quite otherwise. But truly I could not remember. So I sat and looked at them both, and knew that my brother was looking for no phalarope, but for something that he had lost, twenty, thirty years ago, God knows, I do not know.

*   *   *   *   *

When he got home there was a letter under the door, and he knew it was from the captain. He opened it and inside it was a letter from Nella, and a note from the captain, which said, *Thought you'd like to have this tonight. H.M.* For our post comes late in Venterspan, and the captain always got it from the Post Office box. And the captain must have seen that this was a letter from Nella, and he had thought to bring it round, which shows you what kind of man he was. And I give you first the letter that my nephew had written to her, to the farm Vergelegen.

*   *   *   *   *

. . . and when I come home I switch on the lights and put a match to the fire, for the nights are getting cold. But even if I switched on all the lights and had a fire in every room, there'd be

something missing from the house. Sometimes I look at the stamps, and I smile when I remember what you said about them, for they look just like bits of paper when you are not here. I go to Mother's sometimes, and sometimes to Kappie's. Father isn't well, and is like what the English call, a bear with a sore head; but he's all right when Sybrand comes, and they have a drink of brandy and tell their jokes. Kappie plays me music and gives me coffee, good coffee, but not so good as a certain woman makes. He always calls me lieutenant, and one day I want to tell him to call me Pieter, and see what he will do. He will rub his hands, and look very shy, and probably say, thank you, lieutenant, as though I had given him a block of Cape triangulars.

The rugby is in full swing. We played Sonop on Saturday, and beat them 27–3. Good, not so? It was the dominee that did the damage. They just can't hold him. He does that shift on the leg, and suddenly has the whole field to himself. I still hope he may play for South Africa; his heart would burst. By the way, that's not the only damage that he's done. A certain young girl with the name of van Vlaanderen goes about sighing and blushing all day long. But don't say a word.

Tante and Japie are as close as thieves in Social Welfare. She's always in the butcher shop, and he says Ta' Sophie this and Ta' Sophie that, and she pretends to be angry. If you ask me, Japie is interested in Veronica, and you remember he often said he must marry an English girl and join the English church, so that he can play tennis on Sundays. But he has also said the girl must have money, and I think he's still finding that out.

I cannot tell you how I miss you and the children. I look for the day when you are back again, and think about it at nights before I go to sleep. When you come back, that first night I'll have no meetings, no stamps, no rugby, no visitors. And I shall kiss every part of you, from your head to your feet. We'll go to bed early, so that afterwards we can talk. I shan't even smoke, I suppose. I'll somehow convince you, and I know you're not convinced, that my love of you is a love of everything about you, and not just a love of your body. And perhaps one day when you are convinced, and know that my love of your body is part of my love of you yourself, and when you are no longer afraid of it, and accept it truly, and know that such love is no enemy, then perhaps I shall tell you more about myself, for you do not know it all. And if I knew your love was sure for ever, I should not fear to tell you, in fact I should wish to tell you. Then our love would be complete, and nothing would be hidden by one from the other. I believe too that you would then give me more sweetly of your body (I mean more sweetly than you do, which is almost enough already) not because you wished to be kind or suffer me, but because you too would wish to do so. Then I would be in heaven, and safe from all the dangers I told you of, and the angers and ugly moods, all the things I try to tell you about, but I am a fool in telling.

Look after yourself, sweet love, and come back well and strong; and take a big kiss for yourself, and one for Frikkie and one for Grieta. And give Frikkie a good smack on the bottom for me in the bath, not a hard one, just a good one, and then kiss it better. And give my love to Pappie and Ma, and all the family, and all the relations, but don't ask them all to come and stay with us. And don't dare to bring one of the family back that first night. Don't worry about me; Johannes looks after me well, and gives me a clean tablecloth every meal, ha, ha.

You have my love for ever,

Pieter.

P.S. Anna is having a wonderful holiday, and I am beginning to fall for her in a kind of big way. So you'd better hurry.

*   *   *   *   *

Yes, that was the letter he wrote to her, the letter she showed me after we had been destroyed. For then and then only did she understand. Strange it is, that to me who would have given half my life to have had such a letter from a man, no such thing was given; and the one to whom it was given, did not want it or understand it, and wished it never written. For this is what she wrote, amongst other things.

*   *   *   *   *

The long part of your letter I cannot answer fully now, but we shall talk about it when I get home. But even if I hurt you, I must tell you that it hurts me that you think my love is not complete and sure, and that I do not accept the kind of love you write about. Or do you think that Frikkie and Grieta came straight from heaven? Yet it seems to me that a woman's nature is different from a man's, and that for a happy marriage each must give up something, which I try to do. As for these dangers, I think you imagine them, and they are not there at all; for sometimes I think I know you better than you know yourself. But do not worry; three weeks will soon go and I'll be home. I think about you too, every day, and when I go to sleep at night; and though I have the children that is not quite the same. I have given them your kisses and tonight in the bath I shall . . .

*   *   *   *   *

And he sat and read her letter with a face of stone.

XVIII

And that next day he was in the black mood, what we call the *swartgalligheid*, which is the black gall. And the heart is black too, and the world is black, and one can tell oneself that it will pass, but these are only words that one speaks to oneself, for while it is there it is no comfort that it will pass. One could as easily go to the young widow who has just put on her weeds, and tell her that before the year passes she will be laughing in another's arms. For who knows the *swartgalligheid* better than I, though I knew it worse when I was young? Sometimes it lasts for a morning or a day, and will suddenly lift for no cause at all, or when someone says a word of praise or kindness; and sometimes it will not lift for any word at all, and poisons all, food and sleep, and even friends and love. But it came to me less often now, because my life was at the turn; and maybe it would have left me altogether, and I would have gone into my peace, even as the winter veld, when the smoke goes up straight and still into the windless sky, and the whole world lies silent under the sun. Maybe it would have done it at this

very time, but for the bold look of a girl; and I tried to remember if he were looking too, because that would have
made it otherwise, but I could not remember.

So it was in the black mood that he went into Kappie's
store, on his way to work. And Kappie saw at once that it
was the black mood he was in, and tried to joke and make
him smile, but the dark face stayed hard as stone.

— It's music you want, he said.

— Music?

— Yes, music, lieutenant. At half-past seven I play the
Moonlight, and we put out the light, and after that we have
some coffee.

And then he felt a fool, because the dark face stayed
hard as stone, and he felt like a man who offers treasure and
it is scorned. For he was afraid of the lieutenant in his ugly
mood. Yet though he was afraid he would not desist.

— You'll come, he said.

— I'll come, said the lieutenant.

Then the lieutenant went out of the store and down van
Onselen Street to the Police Station, and the street was full,
or as full as our street can be with the children going to
school, and the young men and the girls going to their
offices, in the sharp air and the lovely sun of the highveld
autumn months. And the schoolboys turned, as they always
did, to see the great Pieter van Vlaanderen, who might be
Captain of the Springboks this very year.

Then he went into his office and waited for the inspection. And he vowed to himself he would say no word to the
sergeant in this evil mood, not even if the cells were filthy
beyond all reason, and the yellow seeds of maize were lying
in every door. Then Sergeant Steyn came for the inspection,

and the lieutenant greeted him civilly, and they went out to the yard. And the first thing that the lieutenant saw in the yard was the native prisoner Kleinbooi, who should have been that day in the court at Sonop for a case.

* * * * *

And I stood still and looked at Kleinbooi, trembling with anger. And I told myself I had vowed to say no word to Steyn in my ugly mood. But this was beyond all reason, for there was everyone in Sonop waiting for the case, the magistrate and the police, and witnesses and lawyers. But I stood still and tried to control my trembling, so that I could speak in a quiet voice. Then I said to Steyn in the quiet voice, were you not instructed to send Kleinbooi to Sonop today? And the sergeant looked at me with apprehension, and said uncertainly, Lieutenant, that was for tomorrow. Get the instruction, I said.

While he was away getting the instruction I told myself I must keep quiet, because I was in the evil mood, and because who knew, perhaps I had put down tomorrow, or perhaps I had put Tuesday the sixteenth instead of Tuesday the fifteenth. But when he came back with the instruction I could see he was full of fear. He started to speak, but I said to him, give me the instruction.

And the instruction was for Tuesday the fifteenth, and I saw it was beyond all reason. So I said to him in English, which I know he does not like, and using words that I almost never use, God damn and blast it, can't you read? And then I said, not even Afrikaans? And when he did not answer, I shouted at him, answer me. So he began to answer me in Afrikaans, and it is a rule in the Police, if you force a man to it, that he must answer in the language in which he is addressed. So I shouted at him, answer me in English. So he said to me in English with now not fear but

murder in his eyes, I can read. That's wonderful, I said, who would
have known?

And I was trembling and shaking, with all the strength gone
out of me, and I felt that all the blood was out of me, so that I
was weak as a child.

— Telephone Sonop, I said in Afrikaans, and tell them that
Kleinbooi is being sent at once. Take the car, and go yourself, or
send anyone you like. But do it at once.

— Yes, lieutenant.

When he had left me I went to my office, and shut the door,
and sat in my chair. I sat there for an hour or more, and did no
work, for I had no strength to lift even a pen; and there was a sick
feeling in my stomach and throat, and my eyes were burning.

* * * * *

Ah, how easy it is to speak such bitter words, but they
can never be recalled. I was told by Head Warden van den
Bos how a prisoner escapes from prison, even the strongest
prison in the world. For a warder, he said, must have eyes
for a thousand things, but a prisoner has eyes for only one;
and a warder looks to see that a thousand things are
safe and closed, but a prisoner looks only for the one that is
unseen and open. And that is the only thought of all his
nights and days, and that is how he finally escapes. So the
sergeant had only one thought and only one purpose, and
that was to destroy the lieutenant. Therefore he saw the one
unseen and open thing, in a street safe and sure, with the
people all about, and cars moving, and the sun shining; thus
under the sun and in the open day, the secret was made
known to him, not as knowledge, but as a thing that might
be so, a thing that might be so one time in a thousand, so

that others would pass it by, except the one who has hatred in his heart. And with that knowledge the sergeant struck the lieutenant down, because one was a lieutenant and one was a sergeant, because one took the red oath and one would not, because one was in authority and spoke words in the black mood that even God can not recall.

And when he had sat there the hour, and the strength was coming back to him, Japie came to see him, with the case full of papers that he likes to take about.

— Old brother, I've got Stephanie another job.

— Where?

— With old Louis Griesel and his wife.

— And you told them all about her?

— Every word. But they'll take her, for the sake of our Lord, they said.

And the lieutenant smiled, the first time that day, and he said to Japie, Japie, you're a good fellow.

And Japie fiddled with his papers, and said, you take the black nation too much to heart.

— Old brother, he said, if I took them too much to heart, I wouldn't get any peace.

— I was sitting here in my office this morning, said the lieutenant, and a little bird came and sat there, right on the sill.

— So you were pleased, said Japie, and all kinds of poetry came into your mind.

— No poetry came into my mind, said the lieutenant. And the little bird said to me, the lady's name begins with a V.

Japie blushed, then he got up and shut the door.

— I'm telling you the truth, he said, I'm feeling something. Mind you, old brother, I've felt it before. But not so strong, Pieter, not so strong.

— Has she money, asked the lieutenant.

— That's the funny thing, said Japie. That's why I know it's strong, because she hasn't any money at all. And there's another reason I know it's strong, because her father is an Empire man, and has the King and the Queen in the *sitkamer*. So every time I go there I have to look at them.

— Do you look at them much?

— Well, not so much. But I have to look at the old man, and he thinks Cecil Rhodes had a pair of wings under that black jacket of his. And he doesn't call me Grobler, but *Grobbler*, which sounds to me like a kind of turkey in a yard. How's Nella?

— She says she's feeling better. I had a letter last night.

Japie sighed.

— As the English say, *absence makes the heart grow fonder*. It's true, old brother. I want to see that girl every night. But I can't, because if I do, they'll think I've made up my mind.

Then he laughed his laugh, and it could be heard through the whole Police Station.

— You'd better not do that, said the lieutenant, or you'll have the captain in.

Japie was quiet at once, and he got up at once and picked up his case.

— I'll go, he said.

— I was teasing you, said the lieutenant. He's out.

— I don't like these silent men, said Japie. In any case, old brother, I must go. And don't you worry about the girl

Stephanie, or any other of the black nation. I've got them on my heart too.

He put his hand on his heart to show it.

— Ladies and Gentlemen, he said in English, I pledge myself to the cause of Social Welfare, and will devote to it all my gifts and powers, to uplift the poor and succour the distressed, hoping thereby to purify our human society, that . . .

— I've got to work, said the lieutenant.

— You've got no feeling for language, said Japie.

So he went, and left the lieutenant with the black mood a little lifted. He went home for lunch, and ate it sitting in the garden in the sun; and when he went back, worked hard till the captain came into his room. He stood up, and the captain did not tell him to sit down.

— Coetzee phoned from Sonop, said the captain, and complained that Kleinbooi didn't get there till nearly eleven o'clock.

— Yes, sir.

— Why was that?

— My instruction was overlooked, sir.

— A written instruction?

— Yes, sir.

— If there's one thing above all that I hate, it's to promise a man for nine o'clock and deliver him at eleven o'clock. That means you had to send the car, I suppose?

— Yes, sir.

— Did you make a note of it yourself?

— No, sir. But I remembered it as soon as I saw the man.

— It was pure accident you saw the man. He might have been out working, you might have been out yourself.

— Yes, sir.

— Next time make a note of it yourself. You can't leave such matters to a sergeant.

— Very good, sir.

The captain went out, but he had hardly taken two paces in the passage before he returned.

— It's the one thing above all else that I hate, he said. Duty's duty, and it must be done. One can't put such a thing on to another man.

— Yes, sir.

So the captain went again, and came back again.

— Someone will have to pay for the car, he said. I suggest it's fair that you divide it between you.

— Very good, sir.

And this time the captain went out and did not return. And when the lieutenant was sure that he would not return, he sat down in a black and angry rage, for never before had the captain spoken to him like that. He thought he would go to the captain, and refuse to pay, because he had given a written instruction, and what more could be done than that? And why should he pay for the mistakes of a sullen man that hated him with such bitter hatred? He got up from his chair, and walked down the passage to the captain's office, to tell him he would not pay, that he would rather resign than pay. The captain's door was open, and he would have gone in and spoken God knows what words, but he heard the sound of Dominee Stander's voice in the office, so he did not go in. He went back and shut his door and sat down in his chair, and pulled some papers to him; then he took the papers and flung them across the room. Then he shouted in English, *God damn and blast the bloody Police.* He took out his pipe, and bit it with such anger that his teeth went through the stem, and it was one of his favourite pipes. He took the two pieces of it and flung them across the room also, then he stood up and picked up the papers, saying to himself, *damn the bloody papers, damn the bloody papers.*

* * * * *

And the injustice of it climbed and climbed in my throat, that I should have to pay for the sergeant's mistakes. So I got up again and went to the captain's office, and I could still hear the dominee's voice. So I went back to the office and wrote a note to the captain, and this was the note I wrote.

TRANSPORT OF NATIVE PRISONER KLEINBOOI TO SONOP

Sir,

Under no circumstances whatsoever could I consent to pay half of the cost of the above service to Sonop. I issued a written instruction to Sergeant Steyn, and in the absence of any instruction to the contrary, I consider that my duty was discharged. If you find yourself unable to accept this argument, I shall have pleasure in tendering my resignation, to take effect from as early a date as may be possible, so that I may without delay look out for some more enjoyable and remunerative occupation.

   I am, Sir,
    Your obedient servant,
     Pieter van Vlaanderen (Lieutenant).

And never before in my life had I said or written such a thing about the Police, nor had I ever complained, except as policemen do, about the money. But it was true. I could have got a hundred better jobs, with my war record and my rugby. I could have got a job in Johannesburg, in the mines, where they pay high for rugby. And I thought it was a letter in a thousand, that said what it wanted to say, with pride that a man ought to have, and the right kind of respect and anger, and not a mistake in the English that I could see, although they were learned words. Then there was a knock on the door, and young Vorster was there, and the first thing he saw was the two pieces of the pipe. He picked them up and looked at them and said, Ag, lieutenant, you've broken your pipe. And he looked so sorrowful that my mood was lifted.

— Ag, you're clever, I said.

He fitted the pieces together, and said, again with sorrow, it's finished.

— You're cleverer still, I said.

— Have you got another, he said.

— Not here.

— Shall I nip out and buy one, he said.

I made a face.

— I don't like a new pipe, I said.

He looked at me like a conspirator.

— I could nip over to your house, he said.

— Ag, don't worry.

— It's no worry, lieutenant. Just say the word.

— All right, nip over.

— Which pipe, lieutenant?

— Any one but the fancy ones.

So he was off to get the pipe. Then I read the letter to the captain again, and got the red ink and drew two lines across it, and between the lines I wrote,

CANCELLED
GEKANSELLEER

But I thought it a pity that such a letter would never be read.

XIX

When he had finished his day's work, he went out into van Onselen Street, and whom should he meet there in front of the Police Station but our cousin Anna, the one who wears the yellow trousers when she is in Pretoria, and who says she is not married because the only man she wanted married someone else. And I say that she walked about there on purpose in van Onselen Street, waiting for her cousin to come out, but I do not say there was any wrong in it, nor do I think it. It is just what the schoolgirls do, every Saturday morning; they walk up and down van Onselen Street, and will take three hours to buy some stamps at the Post Office and some vegetables for their mothers at Kaplan's store. And to buy these stamps and vegetables it is necessary to put on a Sunday dress, and there they go up and down the street, giggling and turning and looking at the boys, so that that foolish man van Belkum, the one who teaches at the school and talks so much, made some silly plan and had extra classes on Saturday mornings, *to keep the children off the streets*, he said.

But though it is all right for boys and girls, it is hardly the thing for a grown-up woman. And I nearly wrote down here that no van Vlaanderen would do it, but then I remembered, my nice Martha was walking up and down van Onselen Street a great deal now herself. *Ag*, what a time of life, when one will walk hours in a street to have one second of bowing and saying *goeie middag* to a man!

So Anna looked with great surprise when my nephew came out of the Police Station, as though it were the last place in the world he might come out from. And she said to him, Pieter, I'm dying for a drink.

— Come on then, he said. I want a drink myself.

So they went to Abraham Kaplan's *Royal*, and sat in the place where women can go, and talked in English, for that is a fashion of hers, her people having come from the Cape a hundred years after ours.

— What's yours, he asked.

— Brandy and soda, she said.

— What will your father say?

She lifted her bag.

— I've got my peppermints, she said.

For her parents were simple, and when she came in with the smell of peppermints, they thought it was peppermints that they were smelling.

When he ordered two brandies and soda she was surprised, and said to him, brandy for you? In the rugby season too?

— I've had a bad day, he said.

And she was full of sympathy, so that he told her the story of Kleinbooi and the sergeant and the captain, and even brought out the letter that he had written. And when she saw the two red lines, and the red words, CANCELLED, GEKANSELLEER, she laughed with pleasure and put her hand on his arm, and said, Pieter, I adore you. So they had two more brandies to celebrate her adoration.

Then she told him of the misery of her life, and how it was death to spend a holiday in Venterspan, except that he was there; and of the time she had wanted to go to Durban, and her parents were as hurt and unhappy as if she had said she wanted to go to hell, so she had to come to Venterspan after all. And they did not mind her going to Kruger Park, reckoning she would be safe there with the lions. And she was so depressed that they had another two brandies to lift her out of her depression, and he smoked her cigarettes, which was a thing he seldom did.

So they laughed and joked, and he said many things for which she adored him. How many brandies they had I do not know, but it was more than enough, and I shall write down here, even though I do not know, that it was more than he had ever drunk before.

— *Hemel*, Pieter, it's seven o'clock. *Magtig*, what shall I say?

She was at once distressed, for her father may be a simple soul, but he is stern and strict, and has the evening meal at half-past six, summer and winter.

— Thank God I was with you, she said.

Then she started to eat the peppermints. She said to him anxiously, am I sober, Pieter?

— Don't be a fool, he said, you're as sober as I. And seeing her fear, he said to her gently, don't worry. I'll look after you.

They walked quickly in the cold night air to Anna's home,

and he left her there at the gate. She was feeling better, and said to him, it was worth it, Pieter, you gave me a lovely time. Then she leaned over the gate and kissed him, and he watched her go in, quietly and carefully; yet even though she was anxious, she gave him a wave from the door.

Then he walked back home, and turning off van Onselen Street, he bumped against the iron standard at the corner of the fence, and knew he had drunk too much. But he did not care, for the world was good and happy, and the black mood of the day seemed foolishness, and he was full of power. The black boy Richard brought him his food, and he drank the soup but waved away the rest with distaste, for it had been spoiled by the waiting. He waved away the pudding too, and cut some bread and cheese to have with his coffee. Then he went to the cupboard and got out the brandy that Nella kept against sickness, and poured himself a drink. Then he went into the study and got one of the cigarettes that he kept for visitors, and when he had finished the bread and cheese, he sipped at the coffee and brandy, and smoked the cigarette.

Then he went to the telephone and rang up Kappie, and told him he could not come, having had such a day, but that he would come tomorrow. And the time was half-past seven. Then he went up to his room, and took off his uniform, and put on his flannels and his old jacket of the brown tweed. But he did not look at the beds, his or Nella's, nor even the beds of the children. And he put on his overcoat too, and came down again, and locked the front door after him, and stood a moment at the gate.

And the whole town was still and dark, but for the sound that the wind makes in the trees.

And he did not go to van Onselen Street, but away from it, and turned right and right, and crossed over van Onselen Street where it is dark, away from the three pools of light. And he came to the place where the blue-gums are, and the *kakiebos* weed in the vacant ground. And he stood there waiting in the dark, with the mad sickness and the fear.

And there, God forgive him, he possessed her.

XX

And when she had gone, quietly and carefully through the weeds, he stayed there in the dark, and knelt there at the foot of one of the blue-gum trees, and put his head against the trunk, and prayed to God in Heaven. And before each thing that he prayed, he said in a humble agony, *indien ek mag, indien ek mag,* which is, *if I may pray, if I may pray*; so that if it were presumption, and God did not wish to hear his prayers, then at least he might be pardoned for the praying. For he had a vision that a trumpet had been blown in Heaven, and that the Lord Most High had ordered the closing of the doors, that no prayer might enter in from such a man, who knowing the laws and the commandments, had, of his own choice and will, defied them.

And while he was praying, if he might pray, he heard a twig crack loudly in the vacant ground, and was filled with terror. He stayed where he was, like a man caught in a great trap of dark, full of his enemies, with eyes that could see in the blackness, watching and waiting, but doing nothing so that they might torment him. How long he stayed there he could not remember, but though he strained his ears, he could hear no other sound; and if there were a watcher, he was as silent and as still.

Then he fell again to praying, and made sacred vows, that if there were no watcher in the dark, he would give his life to God. And the brandy he would never touch again. And he would give the rugby and his great fame and honour, and be humble and loyal and unknown, if only there were no watcher in the dark. And he would cease tormenting Nella, to give him something that he now saw was selfish and of the flesh. And when his father died, and he received his portion, he would keep half of it for Nella and the children, and half he would give away, if only there were no watcher in the dark.

And how long he stayed there he could not remember, but at last he rose and came out of the vacant ground. And his body and his clothes stank with the *kakiebos*, which stinking was a symbol of his corruption, so that in his going he feared that the stench of it would go through the town, and bring men and women from every house, to find him and know what he had done. He walked slowly away from van Onselen Street, and turned left and left, and came back into van Onselen Street, far from the pools of light, and turned again there and took the broad road that goes into the grass country, south to Natal and Zululand. Then he walked faster and faster, thinking only to get away from the town. He was a mile or more from the town, where the road runs past the farm Verdriet, which is Sorrow, because husband and wife had trekked there a hundred years before, and no sooner did they reach there after the great sufferings than the woman died, leaving the man alone. And there a

car came along the road from Venterspan, and in a moment
he was in terror, and was up the bank and burying his body
in the grass. And had the car stopped, his heart would have
stopped too, but it went on into the dark; and as he lay there
trembling, he thought of his contemptible estate.

Then he climbed through the fence, on to the farm which
is called Sorrow, and sat there amongst the oxen, some lying
down, and some moving and pulling at the grass, and some
standing with the cud, and all at peace after their labour.
And he saw that they were holy and obedient beasts, and .
envied them. And for another thing he envied them too, and
later wrote it down in his secret book.

And he took off his greatcoat, all stinking of the *kakiebos*,
and laid it down in the heavy dew, so that it might be
cleansed. And he lay down in the dew also, also so that he
might be cleansed. Then he thought he would go to his home,
and boil tins of water on the stove, and pour them into the
bath, and wash himself clean of his corruption.

So he stood up soaked with dew, and put on the coat,
and walked fast along the road to Venterspan, and met
neither car nor any human soul. And he renewed his vows,
and was grateful that the stink of the *kakiebos* had gone.

He went through the little gate and up to the door, and
on the door in the dark was a white note fastened double
with a pin. He took it down and let himself in at the door.
He put on the light and looked at the note. It was written
in pencil, in printed letters such as a child would make. And
it said, I Saw You.

XXI

Then was he filled with terror, for the twig that went breaking in the dark. And he forgot the tins of water and the bath, for now his thought was not to be cleansed but saved. He closed his hand over the paper, as though someone might see it in that empty house, and carried it to his study and put on the light and shut the door. Then he looked at the paper but it said the same as it had said before, I Saw You. It was a piece of paper such as any person might keep in any house. It was unruled and clean, with no name on it, nothing at all but three small words, seven letters, enough to destroy a world.

He sat at his desk, and though the curtains were drawn, he held his hand folded over the paper, lest anyone might see. And why not too? For the town was suddenly full of eyes, that could see in the dark of night, and the thoughts that moved in the darkness of men's minds. And he said in an agony, *o God wees my genadig, o Here Jesus wees my genadig*, but now it was another mercy that he sought, not to be saved from sin but from its consequence. And he repeated all his vows, offering double what he had done before,

157

if only he could be saved. Then though it was after midnight, he heard the car in the street and was filled again with terror. He put the note between the pages of a book, and put the book in the bookcase, yet with the fear that if any person had come, he would have gone at once to that book and pulled it out, so strong was its power; and frantically he brought the books of stamps, and laid them out on the desk, yet with the fear that if any person had come, he would have seen at once that the books had just been laid out, and that their very pattern as they lay was not of accident but of design. So he sat down at once, and pulled the book of South Africans towards him, and tried to study them, but could not for listening to the car. And the car stopped, right before the house, it seemed, and he was in a panic till he heard the laughing of young people; then he knew it was the Vosloo girls back from the party at Hamman's farm, and that the car had stopped, not before the house, but half a block away.

Then he went back to the bookcase and took out the note from the book, and brought it to the light on his desk. The words looked as though they had been written by a child, or by some person either white or black not used to writing, or by some person who wrote thus to torment him. And he considered with fear what the next step would be, for surely it would not end with that. Then he prayed and vowed again in the agony, and thought of his wife and his children, and his father and mother and myself, and of his brother and sisters, especially Martha and the young dominee, and the old dominee too, and Nella's father and mother and brothers and sisters, and the captain and the sergeants and young **Vorster** who thought he was some kind of god, and Hannes de Jongh and all the others of the rugby club, and Colonel de Wet who was his colonel in the war and had recommended him for the Distinguished Service Order, and Professor Krige of Stellenbosch who had written to Jakob van Vlaanderen, *you may be proud of your son, who has won himself great honours, and remained quiet and modest.* But his father never told him that; it was his mother.

And he thought of his children with especial agony, for what kind of man would destroy what he had created, and hurt what he had loved?

* * * * *

That I could not understand, that I could so endanger them; therefore I knew the power of my enemy. For had an angel said to me, you may buy this victory, with an eye or a hand, or with both hands and eyes, I would have said, I buy it. Even had the mad sickness been upon me, and an angel had come there with my son, and said, go on and the child will die, I would at once have desisted. But because the child was not there, and no angel brought it there, I risked to do it a harm more terrible than death.

* * * * *

Then he went to the kitchen, and built a fire in the stove, and put the tins of water on. He put his overcoat and clothes on chairs before the fire, and found some scent that Nella had left, to take away the stink of the *kakiebos.*

He went out of the kitchen door, and down the side of the house to the servants' gate. The whole town was quiet and still, but for the distant barking of some restless dog, and the faint movement of the pines. And maybe the watcher was asleep, and would leave him in peace till tomorrow.

Then suddenly he thought that maybe the watcher was now at that very moment in the captain's office or at the captain's house, with the captain more grave than ever; and maybe the girl Stephanie was there too, smiling and frowning, lying and denying, or maybe, God have mercy, admitting and confessing. Or maybe the watcher was in some other house, and they were gathered round him furtively, listening to the story of the shining star that had fallen into the mud and slime. Yet what proof could such a man have had beyond his word, and a few crushed weeds, that might have been crushed by any man?

*　　*　　*　　*　　*

But this was no comfort to me, for if they had come and said to me, this is your offence, then I might lie, but they would know I lied. How often have I myself not been to a man and said, this is your offence; but he has lied, and I, with the little I knew, could do nothing at all. Yet if they came to me, then I would think that nothing could hide from them the whole pattern of my offence, that it would betray itself in my face, my eyes, my hands, in my mouth that trembled, and said some word it had not meant to say.

It would seem to me that every act, every word, every gesture, would fit only and could fit only into the pattern of my offence; that every reasonable man would see it, and I being also reasonable could not deny it.

And if I denied what they could see to be the truth, then something within me would be broken, and I would cry out, or break down and weep, or something within me would break, so that they, knowing that I had never been so before, would know beyond doubt that I lied.

Yet surely I was a fool, for if a man had been to the vacant ground, what magic was there that could tell him who had been there, and who had crushed these weeds?

* * * * *

Then suddenly he thought of the dogs, for they could bring the dogs from Sonop in the hour; and the terror returned to him, even though he knew they must have some scenter for the dogs. And perhaps they had already taken something while he was away. And the dogs would go out along the road into the grass country, to the farm called Sorrow, and there they would turn amongst the oxen, and knowing nothing of a man's penitence and grief, come back and destroy him.

So he went to the room in the yard where the black boy Johannes slept, and knocked on the door. And when Johannes woke at last, and came to the door and stood there shivering, he said to him, did anyone come to the house tonight? And the boy, no one, *baas*. Are you sure? *Baas*, I'm sure. Were you here all the night? All the night. And no one came? No one, *baas*. Think, Johannes, did no one come? No one, *baas*. Goodnight then, Johannes. Goodnight, *baas*.

Then he took the tins of water and poured them into the bath and washed himself from head to foot, especially the parts of his shame. It was now one o'clock, and he went up to his room, and stood looking at the beds, and vowed and prayed again. Then he got into bed and could not sleep, but heard two o'clock strike and three o'clock strike and four o'clock strike from the clock in the tower of the church. Then he fell into a sleep, and dreamed that he was at the top of a hollow tower, with no way up and no way down. And it was not like any other tower, for the walls were hollow too, from the bottom up, and the space between the walls was filled with knives and forks, and the handles of the knives were made of metal not of bone, like they use in a soldiers' camp. And he lay naked on the knives and forks, and they cut his flesh and drew the blood, and down below on the ground his cousin Anna was shouting to him to come down, but he dared not look at her because of the dizzy height, and because the whole tower shook and quivered, as though it might at any moment crumble to destruction.

So he woke in sweat and fear, not knowing for a moment that it was a dream. Then he knew it was a dream, and would have been comforted, but that he suddenly remembered the note, the note; therefore he vowed and prayed, that if only this thing was lifted, he would never sin again. So he heard five o'clock strike and six o'clock strike. Then he heard the boy Johannes moving quietly below in the kitchen, so as not to disturb him, and fell into a sleep.

When he awoke he wondered if he would let the captain know that he was ill, and could not come. But he decided against it, for if the watcher went to the captain, it would not matter if he were ill or not. And if the watcher went to the captain, what would the captain do? Then the great hope came to him that perhaps the captain would send for him privately, and he would confess, and the captain would save him, even as he himself had saved the boy Dick. And the great fear came to him that the captain would do his duty, for Duty was to him like God; and had the captain not said to him, not much more than twelve hours before, *Duty's duty, and it must be done.*

*   *   *   *   *

And I thought to myself, twelve hours! In those twelve hours the whole world had changed, because of one insensate act. And what madness made a man pursue something so unspeakable, deaf to the cries of wife and children and mother and friends and blind to their danger, to grasp one unspeakable pleasure that brought no joy, ten thousand of which pleasures were not worth one of the hairs of their heads? Such desire could not surely be a desire of the flesh, but some mad desire of a sick and twisted soul. And why should I have it? And where did it come from? And how did one cure it? But I had no answers to these questions.

*   *   *   *   *

And the greater fear came to him that the watcher would not go to the captain, but to the sergeant at the desk, and today it would be Sergeant Steyn. He would say to Sergeant Steyn, I want to lay a charge against Lieutenant van Vlaanderen. And the sergeant would pull the papers towards him, eager to hear what it was. And after the first sentence or two he would say to the watcher, come to a private room. And the story would be told to him there, and he would put it down, sentence by sentence, with a heart full of hate and joy. And when it was finished he would say to the watcher, wait here, and do not say a word. Then he would go to the captain and give him the report, and stand there like a soldier doing his duty as though he knew nothing of hate and joy. Then there could be no mercy, for when a charge is made, a charge is made, and once a thing is written down, it is written down; and a word can be written down that will mean the death of a man, and put the rope round his neck, and send him into the pit; and a word can be written down that will destroy a man and his house and his kindred and his friends, and there is no power, of God or Man or State, nor any Angel, nor anything present or to come, nor any height, nor depth, nor any other creature that can save them, when once the word is written down.

* * * * *

Then he got out of his bed and prayed and vowed again. And he thought he was wrong to think there was no power of God or Man or State, for surely there was a power of God, for was there not a story of a man who was caught and surrounded by enemies that wanted nothing but his death and were strangers to all pity? And there was nothing for him to do but kneel and pray. And when he opened his eyes he was alone, and in the whole wideness of the veld no man at all but he himself. They had talked about that at Stellenbosch when he was young; and some said it was an act of God, and some said that the man was crazed with hunger and thirst and that no enemy had ever been there at all. But he liked to think it was an act of God, and that God could do it now, even when he was surrounded and at the point of death. Then he wondered how God might do it. And the thought came to him that even now the watcher might be dying, that even now he might be dead; or that the girl Stephanie might have died. Or that that very day the great planes from Russia might darken the sky like locusts and rain down death upon the earth, and all men jump to war, and all crimes be forgotten. Or that the rain and the great black storms might return even when the world was turning to winter, and pour down on the earth day after day, and the Buffelsrivier would rise and rise, overflowing its banks, flooding the location and the town and putting all in danger, so that all the police would be called out, day after day, and all other duties be forgotten. And he himself would work night and day, to wipe out his sin and prove his contrition, and the watcher would relent. Or perhaps he would save the watcher, or his wife or children, and he relent. Or perhaps if there were no other way, the watcher would be drowned.

Thus in his misery he would have filled the earth with death, if only he could be saved; and he who asked God's mercy would have had it at the cost of any man or child or nation. Therefore he repented, and asked forgiveness, and left it in the hands of God, whose knowledge is not known to any man; so he was comforted by the knowledge of God's power. He rose to his feet, and by this very rising was filled again with misery, not seeing anything that God could do.

Then he bathed again, from his head to his feet, and went down to breakfast, and tried to be cheerful to the boy Johannes. But he thought only of the note, the note, with the three small words and the seven letters that could destroy a man.

Before he left for the Police Station he went to the kitchen and said to the boy Johannes, I had a feeling someone was here last night. And the boy said, no one, *Baas*. And the lieutenant said, there are always *skelms* about (and a *skelm* is an idle person, who will not hesitate to break the law, but the truth is that in Venterspan we have hardly any *skelms*, and they are mild enough, loafers and pilferers, nothing like Johannesburg).

· Then he took up his lieutenant's stick and cap, and went out to the gate, and stood there a moment before he opened it, and walked with fear towards van Onselen Street.

XXII

But there was nothing to see in van Onselen Street. The whole town lay in the morning sun, and the great tower of the great church stood over it as it had always done before. One of the young rugby boys gave him a swift smile, and said, *see you this afternoon, Pieter,* as though the world was safe and going on. Abraham Kaplan was standing outside the *Royal,* and smiled at him too and said, *I hear you've been drinking all my brother's coffee.* And all the black people from the location moved about the street, and it did not look as though they had any secret knowledge. And Sergeant Steyn was at the desk in the front office, and stood up and greeted him without a smile, and though this morning it pained him, yet every morning it was so; for how could you smile at a man who the day before had said to you, *God, damn and blast it, can't you read?*

So they went through the inspection without a word of enmity, yet the enmity was there as always. He could have said to the sergeant, let me humble myself, and declare that I am no longer your enemy, and let you yourself forgive me for my words. But how can one say such a thing?

He went into his office but did not shut the door. For if there was doom to meet, and the watcher came to the captain, no door would shut it out, and one might as well bear it before it must be heard. But the whole morning no one came. When it was time to go to lunch he went down the passage past the captain's office, and the captain was standing in the office with his hands in his pockets doing nothing but look at the floor. So the lieutenant forced himself to say, *good afternoon, sir,* but the captain neither looked up nor smiled, nor said a word. And the lieutenant thought that the watcher had been after all, and went home with the terror all renewed.

He would not sit in the garden and eat his food, though the boy Johannes had laid it there, because he was in an agony that mocked the trees and sun, and because there seemed some kind of safety in the house. Nor could he eat the lunch, but drank many cups of coffee; and his pipe he lit and put away, and went for the visitors' cigarettes, and sat smoking them, inhaling them into his lungs, which was not his habit. And he listened to every footstep that went past, because perhaps the captain would rather come to the house, and spare him some of his shame. And he went to the study and shut the door, and took the book out of the bookcase again, and because the windows were open and the curtains pulled back, he went into a corner of the room, and took out the note and looked at it, but it told him no more than it had told him before, that he was in peril greater than any death. And in the corner of the room he prayed and vowed again, to give all that he possessed if only the watcher would not tell.

Then he put the paper in the book, and the book back

with its fellows, and thought with the first shadow of a comfort that he had had, that now it looked more of an ordinary book. Then he took the lieutenant's cap and stick, and went out to the gate, and walked with fear towards van Onselen Street.

But again the world was sunny and laughing, and the clean young boys and girls smiled at him in the street, so that he had some comfort. Then he drew in his breath like a man suddenly stabbed with pain, and the marks of pain came between his eyes, for he had remembered the note, the note.

Young Vorster was at the desk when he went in, for the sergeant had not yet returned, and the boy stood up. And the lieutenant put down his hat and stick on the counter, and leaned on it.

— What's it like being in charge, he said.

And the boy looked on the floor and said, with no smile at all, it's all right, lieutenant.

Then the lieutenant was filled with fear, and could not think of another word to say, and he picked up his cap and stick and the boy turned and looked at him with a strange look of some distress, and looked away again, and then stood like a soldier on parade, for a soldier on parade stands stiff and straight, and does not look at any man at all, and if he has grief or hope or anger or contempt, it does not show.

So the lieutenant went to his office and sat in his chair. And he thought beyond all doubt that the watcher must have told this boy, for the boy smiled at him always with shyness and admiration. And the whole of that afternoon he sat in the room with his fear. And it came to him, ask and it shall be given, and search and it shall be found, and knock

and it shall be opened, if it be with a man's whole heart.
Therefore with his whole heart he asked and searched and
knocked, in the room with his fear, till it was time to go to
the rugby.

*   *   *   *   *

And it was there at the rugby I saw him again, who had
not seen him these two whole days. He was grave and silent,
and stood there like a man in authority, with Hannes de
Jongh and the young dominee. He waved to me and Martha,
and I thought he looked fine and true and myself a fool for
my fears. For he did not play, as so many others did, in a
smelling jersey and dirty shorts, but always in a clean white
jersey, and white shorts shining from the iron. So that a
stranger once said to me, who is the man in white, and I
said, with the pride hiding in my voice, it's my brother's son,
Pieter van Vlanderen. And the stranger said, of course, of
course, and then he said again, of course, of course, in such
a way that I would have favoured him, had I ever met him
again.

But of his agony I knew nothing at all, nor that he
watched the boy Vorster with such eyes. For sometimes on
the field the boy Vorster said to him, when some chance
came and they were perhaps waiting for the ball, how am I
doing, lieutenant? And the lieutenant would say, Ag, you
could be worse, and send the boy into some heaven of de-
light; for he was always smiling on the field, and ran every
night when there was no practice, except Sundays, and came
back red and sweating to his bath, and all to get a place in
the lieutenant's team.

Yet this day the boy was silent and withdrawn, and stood

apart and did not smile and did not speak on the field at all. But I did not see it with my eyes. I knew it only when I read what was written down in prison.

And I said to him after the practice, are you coming tonight?

— No, I'm going to Kappie's.

— *Ag*, I said, you were there last night.

— I didn't go, he said.

— So we must suffer, I said.

He smiled at me.

— I'm coming tomorrow, he said.

— You haven't forgotten the picnic?

— I haven't forgotten, he said.

— We won't go anywhere near the pan, I said.

He smiled at me.

I dared to say to him, why don't you smile more often? Then I wished I had not said it, for it wounded him in some secret place. He looked at me and looked away, and he could not hide from me his look of grief, though no one would have seen it but I. Therefore my fears returned to me, though whether it was this thing or something other I could not have said, but I knew it was a thing of fear.

So we walked back together from Slabbert's field, he and Martha and I, and Hannes de Jongh and the young dominee. And the young dominee walked with Martha, and teased her about this and that, so that something came shining into her face and eyes. And I wondered if my nephew saw it too, but I did not know that he saw but one thing with his eyes, and that was young Vorster walking ahead of us. For young Vorster never walked ahead of us; he always walked with his lieutenant, but this night he walked back alone.

When he had got home and had his bath, he trifled with the food that the boy Johannes brought to him.

And the boy said, *Baas*, the *baas* isn't eating his food.

— I'm not hungry, Johannes.

Then he said to the boy carelessly, What's the talk amongst the black people, Johannes?

So the boy told him of this and that, but nothing of any account.

— And how is the old woman Esther?

And Johannes said to him, she's very old.

So they talked about the old woman Esther, and they talked round and about her, so that if there had been anything of account, the boy would have told him. But never once did the boy mention the girl Stephanie. And the lieutenant thought himself a fool, for the boy, though his home was in the location, lived in the room behind the lieutenant's house, and what would he know at all? Yet a man in despair catches at any straw.

— Johannes, fetch me the cigarettes.

Johannes fetched the cigarettes, and when he came back he said, has the master given up the pipe?

Then he went to Kappie's, and they played the Moonlight Sonata, but Kappie says that the lieutenant did not listen to the music, but betrayed again and again the deep agony of his soul. And Kappie noticed the cigarettes, and the movements, and when there were no movements, the pain of the dark eyes. And he would have given anything to speak to the man that he loved, but he was afraid, as a man wishes to go in and takes a step to go in and dare not go in to the room of some great man.

Then the lieutenant returned, and heard in his bed the

clock of the great church striking, eleven o'clock and twelve o'clock. So the first day of the terror passed. But not the terror, for he heard the clock strike one o'clock and two o'clock and three o'clock before God's mercy gave him sleep.

XXIII

And the second day of the terror was as bad as the first, from the time that he took his cap and stick, and stood for a moment at the gate, saying to himself, *Protect me this day, oh God most merciful,* and then went into the street like a man going from safety into the danger of the unknown, and walked with fear towards van Onselen Street.

The boy Vorster was at the desk when he came in, and stood up and acknowledged him, with no smile but a drawn and unhappy face, like a man who has taken great steps for God and has publicly given his life and his possessions, and then finds that he no more believes in Him. So with a heavy heart the lieutenant went to his room, and there found some safety as he did in his house, within four walls where he could see no eyes and hear no voices and be given no rebuffs.

He went to the inspection, and if he saw anything, he said nothing. For had he said one word, however light or careless or generous, it might have loosed on him the hatred of a man who even now might have concealed on him a weapon, given to him by the watcher, that could destroy him. Therefore he

173

would have suffered all. And the captain was still in the silent mood, and nodded to him as briefly as he would have done to any man.

But that very morning came the most frightening thing of all. He had to go to Labuschagne, at the Garage and Service Station, about some trifling thing; for the garage building was very small, and Labuschagne had got into the easy habit of taking out all the cars every morning and putting them into the street, and bringing them all in again at night. And lately he had got into the still easier habit of leaving them out both day and night, and the lieutenant went to tell him that it was favour enough that he should put them out in the day, but at least he must bring them in at night. He spoke courteously to Labuschagne, not as policeman to offender but as friend to friend; and Labuschagne was obliged for the lieutenant's courtesy, and gave him a cup of coffee, and promised not to offend again. Labuschagne was so friendly that it could be seen that he had no secret knowledge, and the lonely and anxious lieutenant was for a moment lifted up, but no Labuschagne would ever have heard the drawing in of the breath of pain, or seen the mark of pain come between the eyes, when the lieutenant suddenly remembered the note, the note, and knew there could be no lifting up.

Then he left Labuschagne and walked back along van Onselen Street, and there was old Herman Geyer standing at his gate, for he like my brother had left his farm to his son and come to the town, and often stood at his gate, wanting the chance of a talk.

So the lieutenant called out cheerfully, *goeie môre*, Meneer Geyer, it's a lovely day today.

But old Geyer did not answer him with any word. He took the pipe from his mouth, and spat with anger and contempt. Then he turned his back to the lieutenant and walked up the path to his house.

Now one can imagine many things in fear. For a boy's silence and withdrawal may be because of some trouble of his own; and your captain's silence may be because he is always silent. But when a man does not answer, and spits and turns, what other thing can that mean? So the great waves of fear rose yet higher and higher, and all his strength was drained out of his body, and his face was white as death, so that it would have been God's mercy for him to die. He was afraid he might stumble and fall there in the street, so he went into our little park, which is no park at all but only a piece of the grass country fenced in and planted with trees, and there he sat on a seat and said, God have mercy upon me, O Lord Jesus Christ have mercy upon me. And all the people went by in the street, and saw only the lieutenant taking a few moments from his duty to sit on a seat in the park, and did not know it was a man in agony, calling on God for mercy. For to them the sun was shining, and the doves were calling in the trees, and they had no trouble greater than General Smuts or the Government, or the rumour that the black people were planning a great strike and procession in Johannesburg.

Then he forced himself out of the safety of the park into the danger of the streets, and walked in fear to the Police Station, and saw again young Vorster silent and unhappy, and sat himself down again in the safety of his room. Then at one o'clock he forced himself out of the safety of his room and again into the danger of the streets, but he could not face old Herman Geyer's house, and he turned down one of the other side streets, and turned left and left till he reached the safety of his house, which was a thing he could not remember to have ever done before. And he would not eat in the sun, but in the house; and he would not eat at all, but drank many cups of coffee, and smoked the cigarettes. And again he said, what's the talk amongst the black people, Johannes? But the boy could tell him nothing of account.

Then he went to his study, and did not take out the book with the paper again, for nothing could alter it. But he vowed and prayed, and longed for the war with Russia, or for the rain, that the rain would come down from the black and heavy sky, that would not open fitfully and show the sun but would be for ever heavy and black, day after day, week after week, pouring down out of lightning and thunder such water as had never been seen before, sweeping away the world, and all men's miseries, and past offences, flooding the world so that when it recovered no man could remember what had been before. Or that the watcher would die, or that the girl Stephanie would die. Or that all else failing, he would die.

* * * * *

That was the first time I had thought of my own death, but I shrank from it, not because I was afraid to die, but because it seemed to me to be the one unforgivable thing, the destruction of God's body, and the doubt of God's mercy. And perhaps even yet some miracle might happen, though what I could not see. But so pitiful was my state that I went again to the book, and took it to the dark corner of the room, and took out the note, hoping that by some great mercy the words had changed. But it said, I SAW

YOU, *even as before. So I began to think I might kill myself, if* there were no miracle.

* * * * *

Then he forced himself out again into the street, not towards van Onselen Street and past Herman Geyer's house, but away from van Onselen Street and then right and right, and back again into the safety of his room. And the day passed slowly and in agony.

That night he came to us, dark and silent and drawn, and we sat there at the meal, he and his mother and sister and I, and his darkness and silence hung like a pall over us, over his mother and me. For the young girl was in love. After dinner we went to my brother's room, and my brother was in low spirits and sombre, and read to us from the tenth chapter of Job. And you may ask why I remember that, for my brother read from no plan, but of his choice and will. Yet I remember it because it is written there—

* * * * *

Wherefore hast thou brought me forth out of the womb? Oh that I had given up the ghost, and no eye had seen me! I should have been as though I had not been; I should have been carried from the womb to the grave.

* * * * *

And I remembered that I had said, out of some childish mood, I am angry that I was born. And I remembered that he had said, out of some deep dark grief, it's I that should be angry that I was born.

Yet it was not only I that remembered what my brother

had read, but he also. For it is one of the things that he wrote down when he was in prison.

When he went back home we usually fussed over him to the door, and I would make some jest to him, such as, *we never see you when the rugby's on,* or I would say, *don't wear out your welcome.* And his mother would say, *put on your coat, it's cold,* or she would say, *you're naughty not to bring a scarf.* But tonight she said nothing to him, but gave him his coat and scarf, and looked at him with the look of care and love. And I said nothing also, but *goodnight, my child* when he kissed me, full on the lip, as he always does.

And when he had gone I looked at his mother, but she would not look at me. So the shadow fell over us too, the first cloud of the clouds of the storm that swept us all away. Yet she had no thoughts or knowledge of any storm, but only suffered for a child that was in trouble too deep for her to understand; and I think still that she thought it was Nella, and did not understand it. And I, I do not know what I thought, being confused between comfort and fear. So I went to my bed and prayed, and he went to his bed and prayed too, in the safety of his home where there was no safety, but only the striking of the hours that struck a day of terror out, and struck a day of terror in.

XXIV

And the third day of the terror was the worst, not because neither the captain nor the boy Vorster would smile or speak to him, but because Herman Geyer had spat and turned; and again he went through the back streets, and would not go past Geyer's house. And still the boy Johannes could tell him nothing of account.

And he could not endure any longer to be tormented, and he thought he would go to the captain and ask him why he was so cold and silent. But suppose it were some other thing, some private thing that the captain kept for himself alone, and suppose the captain turned to him cold and angered, and said to him, van Vlaanderen, you forget yourself, be so good as to return to your duties.

Therefore when young Vorster came to his office with some papers, he said to him, sit down, and the boy sat down stiff and silent, as though he sat down because he was commanded, but would not from choice have sat in the room of such a man. Then the lieutenant went through the papers, but he saw that the boy would not look at him, but sat looking at the table, all stiff and silent.

Then the lieutenant, still looking at the papers, said to the boy carelessly, what's the matter, Vorster?

But the boy did not answer him, and the lieutenant went on looking at the papers.

— I asked you what was the matter, he said.

— There's nothing the matter, lieutenant.

And the lieutenant, greatly daring, said to the boy, that's not true.

Then he said, you're unhappy.

Then he said again, with a slight note of authority that he dared to put in his voice, you're unhappy.

Then he said again, there's something on your mind, but you don't want to tell me.

And the boy looked at him briefly and said, that's true. Then he looked away again.

Then the lieutenant, like a man going into the deep waters, said to the boy, you can tell me.

And the boy said, it's a terrible thing to tell.

And the lieutenant said in a low voice, how terrible?

And the boy said in a low voice too, not looking at the lieutenant, very terrible.

And the lieutenant said, is it terrible news that you have heard?

And the boy said, yes.

— How did you hear it?

— In a letter.

And the lieutenant, in torment and anguish, said, may I see the letter?

But the boy did not answer him, and the lieutenant said to him desperately, may I see the letter?

For if there was such a letter, it had better be seen, far

better to be struck down now and destroyed than to live in torment and anguish and yet be destroyed.

And the boy took out the letter, which was loose and not in any envelope, and gave it to the lieutenant. And the lieutenant opened it slowly, with his whole heart breaking. And he saw that it was a letter from a shop in Johannesburg, threatening the boy for twenty pounds. And sitting in his chair he gave thanks to God for this great mercy.

— And you haven't twenty pounds, he said.

— No, lieutenant.

— And you're afraid your mother will know.

— Yes, lieutenant.

— And you couldn't think of one human soul that would lend you twenty pounds.

— No, lieutenant.

So the lieutenant got out his cheque book and wrote out the cheque for twenty pounds. And he gave the boy the cheque, and the boy put down his head on the desk, and said, lieutenant, lieutenant, so that the lieutenant got up and closed the door, and went and stood by the window and let the boy finish with weeping.

When the boy had finished weeping, the lieutenant said to him, you've been in misery.

— Yes, lieutenant.

And the boy told him he had not slept, but had heard the great clock of the church striking, every night, hour by hour; and that he had been afraid that the captain and the lieutenant would hear of his shame, and he dared not go to any person for such a sum as twenty pounds.

He got up from his chair and he looked at the lieutenant out of the shining eyes.

— One day I'll do something for you, lieutenant. I'll never forget it.

And the lieutenant said with a sudden anger, Good God, do you think I'd see you in misery for twenty pounds?

So the boy went out, and no sooner had he gone out than the lieutenant gave thanks again for this great mercy. And he dared to hope that there might be a greater mercy. Yet the hope died in him when he remembered the note, and the way old Herman Geyer had spat and turned. But the hope returned when he thought of the mercy of this boy and his twenty pounds.

Therefore when he went home for lunch, he went by his usual way, and saw old Herman Geyer standing by his gate, waiting for a chance to talk. But it was too late to turn. And when he was near the gate, and his heart was beating, old Herman Geyer turned away from the gate and walked up the path to his house. Then he saw that he was a fool to take such comfort from a trifling thing, and the fear returned to him, so that again he would not eat his food in the sun and under the sky, but told Johannes to take it into the house.

And now, after these days of terror and want of sleep, he was too spent for fighting, and when it was time again to take his hat and stick and venture into the street, he turned away again from van Onselen Street, and turned right and right, and came to the Police Station by the quiet way. And when he crossed van Onselen Street he met Hannes de Jongh, who said to him, are you right for the match? For the match was no ordinary match, but was the Northern Transvaal against the grass country, and the Northern Transvaal breeds a race of giants. And he thought of the match with dread, for if the watcher were to strike, then let him strike now or wait till after the match, for if he were full of malice and evil, he could wait till the day of the match itself; then on one day thirty thousand people would know what Pieter van Vlaanderen had done, and remember him with especial bitterness.

— I'm all right, he said.

And Hannes said, not like a man judging, but like a man a little anxious, is it true, Pieter, that you've taken to cigarettes?

— Ah, one or two.

Hannes de Jongh looked relieved.

— I heard twenty or thirty, he said.

And that was true too, that he had smoked twenty or thirty a day under the stress of the terror.

— One or two's all right, said Hannes, but twenty or thirty's unbelievable, so I wouldn't believe it.

— Danie smoked twenty or thirty a day.

— Danie wasn't a great footballer, said Hannes shortly.

— He was good.

— I wasn't talking about good ones, said Hannes, I was talking about great ones.

And with that he walked on, and the lieutenant went into the Police Station; and that was the afternoon that Japie came to see him. He was carrying the case with all his papers, and he liked to sit down and open the case, and take out all the papers, and look at them without speaking, as though they brought back great thoughts and memories of great transactions, that were very important and too grave to share with his present company. But he was not really a man for vanity, and he would come back to his ordinary self and make you laugh at something. And now he brought out some papers in a cover, what the English call a file, and he looked at it and said ah, and then he looked at the lieutenant and said, the girl Stephanie.

And the lieutenant was in a moment behind his armour, and he said, what about the girl Stephanie?

— She's working well, said Japie. Old Ma Griesel says she's never had a girl like her.

And the lieutenant said, that's good.

— So we hope she'll keep it up, said Japie, then we won't have to touch the child. Mind you, although your Aunt Sophie agrees that we shouldn't touch the child, she thinks I should get the girl away from Venterspan altogether.

— Does she?

— Yes, she does. But what's the point, old brother? Will she do any different anywhere else? But all these people are the same, get this girl away from here, get this *klonkie* away from here, get him anywhere so long as it's somewhere else. They've got no overall picture at all. But you see Tante Sophie has me on the spot, because she knew me when I was a boy, and still thinks she can order me about. You'll have to speak to her, old brother.

And the lieutenant sat and considered it, that he should speak to me about the girl Stephanie.

Japie packed away his papers with a sigh.

— It's a big job reforming the grass country, he said.

— And how's the girl with a V?

Japie was serious.

— It's bad, he said, it's bad.

He looked at the lieutenant gloomily.

— That's why I don't joke any more, he said.

He stood up with his papers.

— Marriage is a serious thing, he said. I've kept out of it so long that sometimes I take fright at the very idea.

He turned to his friend with decision.

— I'm coming to see you one night for advice, he said.

Then he went, but was back again in a moment, putting his face around the door, and the man that did not joke any more was full of jokes.

— How's the girl with an A, he said.

The lieutenant looked at him blankly.

— What girl with an A, he said.

— Anna, of course. Did you think I didn't see you two in the Royal, billing and cooing?

The lieutenant smiled.

Then Japie said, didn't you get the note on the door?

Then he went down the passage laughing his terrible laugh, but suddenly remembered the captain and was silent, and went tiptoeing on. But the lieutenant was out of his chair in a moment, and in the passage too, asking in a trembling voice, what note on the door?

And Japie shook a finger at him, and spoke softly because of the captain, and said, I saw you, I saw you.

XXV

So the miracle came after all. And the twig breaking in
the dark was only the twig breaking in the dark. And the
watcher and tormentor was no watcher and tormentor at all,
but only a joking friend. And the sun was shining and the
doves were calling in the trees, and people had no trouble
greater than General Smuts or the Government, and the
thought of the black procession in Johannesburg. So the
prayers of thanks to God were poured out in the office in the
Police Station.

He came out of the Police Station, past a boy smiling
with adoration, into a street of safety and friends.

Kappie's store had just closed, so he went to the little room
at the back, and said to Kappie in a great voice, what are we
having, tea or coffee? And Kappie, though he was glad that
the lieutenant should treat him so, was amazed in his heart,
because the lieutenant had never said such a thing before, but
would wait till he was asked. And the lieutenant walked
round the small room with smiles and pleasure, and said
pleadingly to the little bird that was Kappie's friend, come

now, won't you sing? Then he went to the books of the records and said, I'm going to my mother's tonight, but tomorrow night we'll have some music. Then he said, none of your sad stuff, Kappie, something cheerful and light, what about a Gilbert and Sullivan?

So he opened more pages of the secret book of his life than Kappie had ever seen, and each stranger than the last, making the book more secret than it was before. But the other knew that the great agony had been lifted.

— How's your wife, lieutenant?

— She's well, Kappie. Do you know what I wrote to her?

— No, lieutenant.

— I wrote to her, one day I'll ask Kappie not to call me lieutenant, but by my name.

And Kappie was embarrassed, and fiddled with the teapot, and said, I couldn't do it, lieutenant.

And the lieutenant laughed at him and said, you're old enough to be my father.

And Kappie said, that doesn't make any difference.

And the lieutenant felt his friend's embarrassment, and said gravely, why, Kappie?

And Kappie shrugged his shoulders, and fumbled with the teapot, and with the words too, and said, respect, lieutenant.

But he saw the sudden mark of pain that came between the eyes. He busied himself with the tea, and poured it out, and they sat there gravely drinking. And Kappie sat there like a man with a puzzle with a hundred pieces, with a picture all but complete, with six or seven pieces that would not fit at all, whatever way you turned them; so that you knew this could not be the picture at all, but that the real picture must be something strange and different, and that the parts that looked complete must be something quite other, if these six or seven pieces were to be made to fit.

Then the lieutenant told him that he had a puzzle too, for why should old Herman Geyer spit and turn. Kappie smiled and said, there could be two reasons for that.

— What are they, Kappie?

— One because you're a policeman, and one because you're a neighbour. You see one of his neighbours complained to the captain about the stables and the flies, so the captain inspected the stables. He told old Herman that he must either build a new stable or send the cows back to the farm, and you know old Herman could not be without his cows, and you know to spend his money is like giving blood. So Herman is very angry with the police and with his neighbours. And you are both policeman and neighbour, so for you he spits.

So the lieutenant left Kappie with still another page of the book, and Kappie sat by himself and thought of the strangeness of his friend, and of the deep agony that had been lifted and the small pain that could still return, and of the tall grave man that went round the room smiling and pleased. And he could not understand it, except to know that it was deep and strange.

And that night my nephew came to our house, and stole behind his sister Martha and put his hand over her eyes, and said in a squeaking voice, guess who it is.

And she said at once, Pieter.

But he said in the squeaking voice, No, guess again.

And she said again, Pieter, and tried to struggle free to look at him, though she might have saved her breath.

And he said, No, guess again.

— I give in, she said.

Then he bent and whispered something to her, so that she went red as fire, and was so angry as such a girl could be. But he laughed at her anger, and walked round our house too, looking with eyes of pleasure at all the things he had seen so many times before. His father, who was now recovered from the influenza, gave him one swift heavy-lidded look, and returned to his paper. But his mother and I watched him with wonder.

And at dinner my brother was jovial too, and told us the story of how he had taken Sybrand Wessels into the Social Welfare Office that was the old butcher's shop, and how he had asked Japie, why do you have that hook? And Japie did not want to tell him, for he knew that the *Oubaas* knew quite well the story of the hook, and though Japie likes to make himself a fool, he does not like others to do it too. And when my brother saw that Japie did not want to tell the story of the hook, he looked at him as he had looked at him on the farm Buitenverwagting, when Japie was a boy, and he said to him again, a little cold and stern, why do you have that hook? Then Japie had to tell them about the hook, and Sybrand Wessels was spluttering with laughter, not because of the story of the hook, but because my brother had already told him how he would force Japie to repeat his joke, and because he knew that the devil was in my brother, and because he knew that the devil and my brother were laughing together inwardly, and because he could see that Japie was embarrassed at having to tell the joke. So the two old clowns laughed at the young one, and the young one the biggest clown of all.

— And now, said my brother, when I go to the Social Welfare Office, Volkswelsynbeampte Grobler is suddenly not there.

Then he grunted at us.

— I'll teach the Government, he said, to give me Japie Grobler for thirty minutes of my time.

Then my nephew said, I'll tell you another story just like that.

And he told us the story of the Duke of Wellington, who when he was old and famous and no longer a fighting man, went one night to his old regiment for dinner; and all the officers were nervous and excited at having so great a man. And the Duke of Wellington told them the story of how on one of his campaigns, his man had opened a bottle of port after the dinner, and there in the bottle was the body of a rat. So one of the officers said nervously, it must have been a big bottle, sir. And the Duke of Wellington looked at him and said, it was a damned small bottle. And the officer said, foolishly and nervously, it must have been a small rat, sir. And the Duke of Wellington looked at him and said, it was a damned large rat. Then he looked round at them all, but no one said another word.

And the story caught my brother under his guard, even though his son used the word *verdomde* which he does not like, so that he suddenly spluttered some of the food in his mouth out onto his plate. And we all laughed, but my brother did not laugh, because he was putting back his guard. He growled, and looked like the Duke of Wellington himself, so that we all laughed more than ever. And you could see that he was secretly proud to be likened to the Duke of Wellington, even though he had been an Englishman. And my sister-in-law watched her son with wonder.

And the next Saturday he went to Pretoria, and there the grass country beat the giants of the North, for the first time in history. And thirty thousand people clapped their hands, and called out, van Vlaanderen, van Vlaanderen. And they called out for the young dominee too, for it was Pieter van Vlaanderen and the dominee that beat the giants of the North. And the young girl went with them too, and came back with her face all shining, having seen thirty thousand people go mad over the two men that she loved.

And I remember that time, for our happiness came back again, like a moment of sunshine snatched from a heavy sky.

And I remember that time, for Sergeant Steyn went for his holiday with his family, to the South Coast of Natal, where all the English people are. And his daughter Henrietta, who was ten years old because the sergeant had not been to the war, collected the small coloured shells that lie on the beaches there. She collected them in her innocence, and put them into a box, and brought them back to Venterspan; and by one of them collected in innocence, the house of van Vlaanderen was destroyed.

XXVI

Then Nella and the children came back from the farm Vergelegen all brown and healthy, for the sun is hot even in winter down there on the edge of the low country. He went to meet the bus in a great excitement but also in a great constraint, for he could think only of the letter, and how he had revealed himself again to her, and how she had again drawn back. While he waited for the bus, which was a little late, he thought that perhaps he should have had a meeting after all, or some visitors, partly to defend himself against her, and partly to show that he was cold and did not care; and he thought of the letters they had written since, full of news, news, news, and the formal words of love. So when she came they kissed, not coldly, but with constraint; and when she came she did not look at him even from the bus, nor come at him with the shining eyes, but shepherded the children and said, look, there's your father.

But the warmth broke out of him nevertheless, at the sight of his children. And he put the small boy into one great arm and the small girl into the other, and pressed them without mercy against his body, and they did not cry out, being used to his ways.

Then they got into the car, and drove to the house, and it was nearly dark, so they put on the lights and pulled down the blinds. And she did not say, it's nice to be home, or kiss him again, but busied herself with the children and the bath, and went about the house as though she were intent on a thousand duties. And so remote was she that he went and stood in the study, and heard the noises of the children in the bath, and heard her say to them, now be good and I'll fetch your *pappie*.

And he thought he would not go, for how could a woman be so blind? He would fling out of the house, and go to the Royal and drink with his friends, and sit with them too, and come back when the house was dark.

Then she came into the study and shut the door, and came at him with the shining eyes, and went into his arms, and said, my love, my love. And he held her with gratitude and hunger, and kissed her mouth and eyes and neck, and put his hands over her breasts. And she pulled down his head and whispered to him, I'm sorry about the letter, so that his joy was complete.

Then she said to him, any visitors tonight?

And he said to her, only three.

And she said to him, I didn't bring any relations.

Then he held her to him again, and kissed her mouth and eyes and neck, and she said to him, but not coldly, be sensible now and come and see the children in the bath.

So they went to see the children and the joy of life burst out of him, so that he pulled them about in the bath, and could have hurt them, but that his strength was gentle. Then he punished his son for being so long away, and kissed him better; then the daughter must be punished too. Then he punished them both for sending him only crayon drawings and no letters; then he punished them both because the bus was late. And they laughed and shouted, and splashed the water all over the room, so that Nella came in and said, you're all naughty to make such a mess.

Then they had their meal, and neither he nor she could eat, being sick of love. The children were put to bed, and the boy Johannes went to his room, and the kitchen door was locked, so that they had the house to themselves. Then she, not he, made for them a bed in front of the fire, which was a thing they had not done since the earliest days of their love. And their joy was so complete that there was not need for any words, save for the words of love. Nor did he need to talk to her about the love which is both of the body and of the soul, nor of the dangers that were all about him; for there was no danger there, nor need have been again, had she had some deeper understanding than she had. And he kissed her feet, remembering, and she remembering also, that the first time he had done it she had wept; but she would not let him stay there, but drew him up to her, head by head, so that they might be equal.

And he said to her, I worship you.

And she said to him, I worship you also, so that the mark of pain came there between his eyes in the dark.

Then she got up and put on her gown, and made coffee for them over the fire. And there was no need to fetch anything, because everything was there already.

She said to him, now's your chance to smoke.

— I haven't even brought my pipe.

— You're in a bad state, she said.

Then she went in her gown to fetch his pipe and tobacco.

When she came back she said, what's happened to your favourite pipe?

— It's broken.

— *Ag*, that's a pity. How did you break it?

— It fell on the floor in the office.

— Careless man, she said, and kissed him.

Then she gave him one of the new rusks, and he said to her, this is the finest rusk that was made in the history of the world.

So they laughed, for so in love can one laugh at the *swartgalligheid* as though it were something of no account. And they talked of this and that, and of the wonderful rugby match in Pretoria, and the girl Martha in love, and she put her hands and feet to the fire, and sat there like a child, which was a thing he loved. Then they finished the coffee, and the rusks, and he put away his pipe, and drew her down again into his arms, and they renewed their love.

Twelve o'clock was striking from the tower of the church when they went up to their room, and he thought to himself with wonder that it was the only striking he had heard that night.

*   *   *   *   *

The next morning he took his lieutenant's cap and stick and went out towards van Onselen Street. Old Herman Geyer was at his gate, and the lieutenant called out to him before he could turn, *Goeie môre*, Meneer Geyer, it's a beautiful day. Then old Geyer turned and would not say a word, and the lieutenant went smiling on his way.

When he entered the Police Station the boy stood and smiled at him with adoration, and Sergeant Fourie said to him, when shall I come for the inspection, lieutenant? And the lieutenant said to him in a great voice, any time you like, of the morning, noon, or night, so that the sergeant looked at him with astonishment and the boy with pride. For Sergeant Steyn had gone on his leave, to the beaches of Natal, where the small coloured shells lie in their thousands on the shore. When he was in his office, the captain came to him, so he stood up till the captain said, sit down, van Vlaanderen.

Then the captain said, I'm going on leave next month.

— Yes, sir.

— I wanted to leave you in charge, but they think you're too young. So they're sending Captain Jooste from Pretoria. Are you disappointed?

— Not very, sir.

— Good. You'll find Jooste a decent fellow. In any case, if they put you in charge, you couldn't run about playing rugby.

The captain did not smile, but suddenly his whole brow lifted, which was a queer trick of his, and was really some kind of smile.

— We mustn't allow duty to interfere with rugby, he said.

Then he walked out of the office saying, about the car, they say we needn't pay for it.

So that day would have been complete, but that the girl went back too soon to the rule and custom. And he knew, both when he went back at lunchtime and when he returned at night, that she was already withdrawing, to some safer ground, to some world where she was safe and sure, not knowing that the world she left was safer and surer, because of that idea that she had, which was good and true and twisted, that the love of the body had a place where it stayed and had to be called from, and how it got called and what called it, God knows, I do not know. And why she should withdraw so soon from such a happiness, God knows, I do not know.

And had he that day been offered any gift, he would have chosen neither honour nor riches, but another night with her before the fire. Ah, how great is God's gift of love, that love which is of body and mind and soul, and why should she who had it, not understand, and why should I understand who never had it? And why should I who understand never have had it? For I would have given, without rule or custom, nor any withholding. And had he been thus given, then I say he would never have been destroyed. For have I not seen a score of times with my eyes, when men and women are denied, how they go seeking? Like a man who is robbed of a jewel, and goes seeking it amongst the dross and filth, and all men look at him with pity and contempt, not knowing of his distress. And did not Maria Duvenage, after twenty years of married life and child-bearing and going to the church, suddenly go off with a worthless scamp, who left her afraid and desolate, so that now she sells herself to any stranger in Johannesburg? They called her by evil names, but I have heard her story, when she sent for me to come to the wattle trees on Buitenverwagting; and even before, I knew her husband for a hard and loveless man, who broke her spirit and enjoyed her flesh, and drove stern and strict in the black Sunday clothes. But may God forgive me if what I write is wrong, and against His laws; for I believe His laws are made in love, and though one does not understand, one should be obedient. And it is because I am obedient that I write these words. Yet, child, I understood you, and every word you ever wrote. And I say to myself, my God, my God, what did he do to be destroyed?

Therefore when he went to the house she was already withdrawn. And that night when they went to sleep she said her prayers and kissed him, and got into her bed. And carelessly he got into his bed too, and put out the light, and lay there alone, yet not alone, for the black mood, the *swartgalligheid*, came and lay with him and listened with him to the striking of the hours.

* * * * *

But you must not think I judge, nor must you think I write as a child and ignorant. For I know there is a time to weep and a time to laugh; a time to mourn and a time to dance; a time to cast away stones and a time to gather stones together; a time to embrace and a time to refrain from embracing. And we eat and drink by rule and custom; and men like my brothers take their liquor by rule and custom, except for the time when he was sick. And to have a feast is good, and to eat and drink and be merry, but one cannot live on feasting. Therefore I cannot judge.

Yet why did she not understand that this was a hunger of the soul, for safety, even if not for love? For I tell you that he would have foregone his fame and honour to have been safe in love; and he would have foregone the holding in respect, and been an ordinary man, if he could have been safe in love. And had he been safe in love, he would perhaps have been less courteous and grave, and held himself less tall and straight, and would have joked a little coarse and rough, and had the faults of ordinary men. They would have said, ah, van Vlaanderen, there's a fellow for you; they would have said, Pieter, you old (with a word they use), come and have a drink. Instead they said, yes, Pieter, or no, Pieter; or yes, lieutenant, or no, lieutenant. And some of them even said, lieutenant, allow me the honour of standing you a drink.

Yet I cannot judge, for where is the end of judging? Shall I judge myself, that should have hammered at the door, and cried out not ceasing? Or shall I judge my brother, that was proud of the boy with the wild horse and ashamed of the girl with the wild flower? Or shall I judge the sergeant for his hate and joy? Or Coenraad Willemse, that put the girl Stephanie into the street? Or the girl herself, who was like a tigress for the child?

And shall I judge the dark unhappy boy, who had such strange and lonely pleasures, and was brave and gentle, and was master of all things save one, and of his choice and will went seeking in the filth? And shall I judge my God, and the Lord of all compassion, who made us all, and filled us with dark strange things, that one goes lawful and obedient, and another is destroyed? Therefore I cannot judge at all, except to wish she had been otherwise.

*   *   *   *   *

So the black mood returned, the *swartgalligheid*. And they quarreled again over some foolish thing. Therefore she sat in a misery, not knowing what could be done, and wishing she were back again on the farm Vergelegen, safe with her father and mother and her children, with a safer kind of love; and hurt too, deep in her soul, that this was the thanks she got for her shy and shining gift. And he flung out of the house in a misery, and walked about the town in his anger and the dark, and went again to the vacant ground and the stinking weed, and broke the law, of his own will and choice.

XXVII

And his terrible knowledge of himself lay in him darkly and heavily, and took away his laughter, and the laughter of his wife, so that the children were the only creatures that laughed in that house. He went to his work darkly and heavily, and he came back darkly and heavily, and played with his children in the bath, because that was his habit, but his wife could hear and see that it was not the same. Yet what could she do but suffer it?

Japie came to him with his case of papers, and said to him, old brother did you speak to your Aunt Sophie about the girl Stephanie, because she is still after me to send the girl away?

— No, I didn't speak.

— It's no use, said Japie. Each community must carry its own weaklings. But your aunt won't listen to me, and if you won't speak to her, what can I do?

— Perhaps, said the lieutenant, it would be better to send her away.

And Japie was angry and said, in God's name, why? But the lieutenant could not answer him.

Then Japie struck the table with his fist and said, under what law?

But again the lieutenant could not answer.

So Japie got up and said, I always thought you were for the black nation. The girl's working, she's working well. Isn't she doing what the magistrate told her to do? Why the devil should she be sent away?

And the lieutenant did not answer. Japie looked at him with irritation.

— Pieter, I don't understand you, he said.

And that was true, that he did not understand, and he went out of the lieutenant's room, wondering why his friend should treat him in this way.

That was the night that the young dominee came to my nephew's house, and asked Nella with that boyish charm of his if he could speak to her husband privately. So the two men went into the room where the books and the stamps were kept.

The young dominee sat down, and he said to the other with his face all shining, Pieter, I'm in love. And the other was desperate that men should come to him with their tales of love, but he summoned all his strength together, and made his face into the fashion of a smile, so that any man could have seen it was no smile, except a man in love.

— Ah, you're in love, he said.

Then he said with the smile, you surprise me.

— Have I any hope, Pieter?

— Are you blind then?

— No, I'm not blind. I think she likes me, Pieter. But I don't wish to presume.

— Haven't you seen her eyes?

— What do you mean, Pieter?

My nephew got up, and walked about the room.

— If we talk about you at the house, he said, my mother

says she likes you, and my aunt says she likes you, and I say I like you. But that sister of mine doesn't know what to do or say; she sits there afraid that someone will suddenly stand up and shout at her, do *you* like him? Then she would run crying from the room.

The young dominee sat there, breathless and enraptured.

— You don't say, Pieter?

— I *am* saying. Didn't you hear me?

— I heard you, Pieter. But I can't quite believe it.

— Do I look like a liar?

Then the young dominee said, no, no, he did not think that my nephew looked like a liar, and my nephew must forgive him, because he didn't quite know what he was saying, because he was *deurmekaar*, which means *all confused*, and he was *onderstebo*, which means *upside down*, and his position was *ellendig*, which means something stronger than *miserable*, and it can better be said that his position was *one of misery*. And he did not know that he might as well have stabbed his friend with a knife, as to say that this rapture was misery.

And his friend said, *ellendig, ellendig*.

And the blind man said, yes, *ellendig*, and went on to explain that the misery was a rapture, and the rapture was a misery, till the other wondered how long he could endure to hear the tales of a man in love.

— And Pieter?

— Yes?

— What about your father?

— What about my father?

— I'm scared of him, Pieter.

My nephew laughed, even as his father laughed.

— You wouldn't be the first, he said.

— Sometimes I think he doesn't like me, Pieter.

— *Ag*, he likes you. Otherwise he wouldn't tease her.

— Does he tease her, Pieter?

— He tells us she's a good girl, always at the church.

And the young dominee went off into a second rapture.

— Shall I ask him then, Pieter?

And my nephew laughed again as his father laughed.

— Who else do you think will ask him, he said.

— That's true, that's true.

— Of course it's true. And when he speaks to you, say *ja* if you mean *ja*, and say it as though you meant it; and say *nee* if you mean *nee*, but don't say, *ja, nee*, because he'll think you're afraid of him.

— But I am afraid of him, Pieter.

— Well, he doesn't know it, and don't you let him know it.

— Thanks for the advice, Pieter.

And my nephew laughed again, and said, *raad is goedkoop*, which means, *advice is cheap*. Then he said, do you want some more advice?

— Yes, Pieter.

— Ask the girl first.

— I was going to ask your father for permission to ask her.

— That's old-fashioned.

— All right, Pieter. And Pieter?

— Yes?

— I've one more thing to ask.

— Yes.

— Would you become a *diaken* in the church?

And my nephew continued to walk up and down the room.

— A *diaken*, he said.

— Yes, Pieter.

— I don't know that I'd like to.

The dominee said, with a gentle kind of reproof, it might be a duty.

My nephew sat down at the table.

— A duty, he said.

— Yes, Pieter. You're looked up to by the whole community. You've been given great gifts by the Lord. Shouldn't these gifts be given back to Him also? Mightn't some young fellow say, there's Pieter van Vlaanderen, and what he does I'll do too?

So Pieter van Vlaanderen put on all his armour, and he looked straight at the young dominee and said, I'm not good enough.

— Ah, it's right to say that. But often when a man says, I'm not good enough to do it, but I'll do it, then he finds he has strength to be better.

— Is that so?

And the young dominee, unconscious of any irony, said earnestly, that's so, Pieter, so that the older man envied him his innocence.

— I'll think it over.

— That's all I ask, Pieter.

— I'll think it over, but I'll promise nothing.

He looked again directly at the dominee.

— I'll have a lot to think over, so I'll take some time.

The young dominee said with admiration, you're modest.

— Modest, eh?

— Yes, very modest.

My nephew laughed his father's laugh.

— You need more than modesty to be a *diaken*, he said.
He stood up.

— Come on, he said. Let's go and tell Nella the news.

The young dominee held out his hand.

— Pieter, wish me luck.

My nephew took him by the hand.

— I wish you luck, he said. But don't worry, he'll say yes.

And they laughed that the one could so easily read the
other's mind. Then the dark ugly wit came into the gentle
man, and he said, tell Nella everything, hold nothing back,
there's nothing she likes better than a tale of love.

*   *   *   *   *

When he had gone, and Nella had gone to bed, I went to my
study and thought over the matter of becoming a diaken. I did
not know if it would help me or otherwise, for if I could break
one sacred vow, why should I be able to keep another? And if I
broke one law, why would two be better? Then I thought perhaps
it would give me a higher duty, and the very highness of the duty
would be a help to me; yet why should a man be able to do a
higher duty when he cannot do a low? I thought of those people
of the early Church, who put upon themselves incredible vows
and sufferings, and went mad, not holy.

And I thought with envy of the dominee and young Vorster,
who had open eyes and faces, so that you could see that nothing
was hidden there at all. Had I not been once like that myself? Or
perhaps I had not, I could not remember. I remember the thoughts
and deeds that troubled me when I was a boy, but I think that is
true of almost any boy. Surely my face was open. Yet I could not
remember. Had I had too great a hunger for praise, so that I turned
in on myself, and hid all my weaknesses? But I could not remem-

ber. Nor could I remember when I became so evil, for I was not evil in the early days of my love.

I sat there in great agony of mind, hungering for my youth, to have it all over again and make it better. I thought of the farm Buitenverwagting, and the simple pleasures I had, and the call of the piet-my-vrou that even today can fill me with thoughts and memories unspeakable. Was I evil then, who had such joy of creation?

I vowed anew that never again would I commit the unspeakable offence, and I decided that I would take no second vow until I could keep the first. And I thought of Nella and Martha and my mother, and my brother Frans's wife, with their simple chastity, and wished to God I had been made a woman.

* * * * *

So the young dominee came to our house, and went off with my brother to the *sitkamer*, leaving his wife and the girl and me to wait with apprehension. For my brother had done strange things to the suitors for his daughters. I have told you that my brother had two kinds of jokes, and one was meant to be laughed at, and one was not; and though we knew the one from the other, the young suitors did not always know. And sometimes one would laugh at the second kind of joke, with the whole family sitting there silent and apprehensive, so that the poor boy laughed alone; then my brother would look at him with contempt in his heavy-lidded eyes, and he would not come again. That was why my niece Henrietta did not marry Dick le Roux, who was a good but nervous boy; that was why she married her silent husband, because he never laughed at all, and one joke was the same to him as any other. He would sit in the house at Buitenverwagting, one

night after the other, as though he were the only person
there. And when Emily's suitor came, the one who carried her
off to Johannesburg, then by the grace of God my brother
broke his leg, and by the time it was better the young man
was like one of the family, and knew all the ins and outs.

Then after thirty minutes my brother came in with the
young dominee, both very grave. And my brother went to his
daughter and said in an unbelieving voice, I hear you want
to leave me. The girl stood up and buried her face in her
father's beard, and said, No, *Pappie*.

— Do you hear that, dominee? She doesn't want to go.

Then the devil came into him, and he said to her, there
now you needn't go so often to the church.

Then he kissed her, and growled at her, I hope you'll be
happy, daughter.

Then he said to the dominee, have you kissed her yet?

The dominee went so red as a man could go, and said,
once, *meneer*. Which I tell you that you may see how the old
fashions still linger amongst some.

And my brother growled, what's the world coming to?
You'd better kiss her now.

Then he went to his wife and kissed her, and said, you
were bolder than that.

And the young dominee went awkwardly to his girl,
but you can imagine the kind of kiss, there in front of us all.

— I won't say she's the best of my daughters, said my
brother, but I won't say she's the worst.

Then he growled at me.

— *Magtig*, Sophie, how long will you keep us waiting for
the wine?

XXVIII

That was the time that the black woman died of the smallpox in Maduna's country, and one sickened in our own location at Venterspan. And I tell you that my sister-in-law and I, and Dominee Stander, and the captain's mother and the captain himself, and my nephew also, were ashamed of our location at Venterspan; for while it is true that we brought Christianity to the dark continent, we brought other things too. And when the smallpox came, some of our people were in a panic. That was a hard time for the police; the doctors and nurses came from Johannesburg and Pretoria, and they worked day and night, vaccinating all the people of the grass country, white and black. Labuschagne fitted up a machine for making lights, and they worked day and night at every sub-police station in the countryside, and on all the farms, and throughout the length and breadth of Maduna's country. And my sister-in-law, who was a true follower of the Lord Jesus Christ, went working in the location herself with two of our servants from Buitenverwagting, cleaning up the filth, and putting stuff into the drains, that are no drains at all but

only the courses that the foul and thrown-out water makes
for itself, before it flows, black and sour, into the Buffelsriver.
And my brother spoke neither for it nor against it, except to
growl at her, *of course I'd like the smallpox in the house.*

And they will tell you about all this time of anxiety and
toil, those who have not lost all sense of justice, that it was
the lieutenant who did it all. It was he who got all the stuff
from Pretoria, and had it sent to this place and that, and
arranged for the cars and the lights, and arranged all the
places and the times, so that there was not one place or time
when the doctors and the nurses and the stuff and the people
were not all there together. And it was he who got all the
black people together, in the locations and down in Maduna's
country, telling them to have no fear, but to suffer this small
scratching of the arm and save themselves from dying. And
they obeyed him because he had the great authority, not
only of his height and rank, but of that strange thing that
lives within a man. But he was weary unto death.

And on the third night, thus weary unto death, he came
back from Maduna's country, and went into his office, and
put a telephone call through to Pretoria for more of the stuff,
for they kept our telephones open day and night while we
fought the smallpox in the grass country. While he was waiting for the call, he put his head down on his arms, but he
was not asleep but thinking, not of the smallpox sickness but
of his own. Therefore he heard the captain come into his
room, and because of his misery, pretended he was asleep.
And the captain put his hand on the lieutenant's shoulder,
and shook him gently, and said, Pieter, it's time you went
home.

Now the captain never called him by this name, nor did

he ever touch a man. Therefore when the captain called him by his name and touched him, as some fathers touch their grown sons and as some do not, and because he was weary unto death and full of misery, therefore he was moved in some deep place within and something welled up within him that if not mastered could have burst out of his throat and mouth, making him a girl or child. Therefore he could not speak nor lift his head nor stand.

And the captain, seeing he was awake, and seeing he was unmanned, and thinking it was the weariness, turned away from him and went and stood in front of the map of the grass country.

Then the lieutenant stood and said, I'm waiting for Pretoria, sir.

— I'll wait for Pretoria. Go home.

The captain went and sat in the lieutenant's chair, and picked up a piece of paper from the table.

— Are these the things you want?

— Yes, sir.

— Go home then. You've done enough for twenty men. Therefore the thing welled up again within him, as though it were something that would not be denied, as though it were commanding him, speak and speak and speak.

— There's something I ought to tell you, sir.

The captain held up the paper and said, something to do with this?

— No, sir.

— Then, said the captain with authority, it can wait till tomorrow.

Then the telephone rang, and he raised his hand in a farewell salute, and took up the telephone. When the call was done, he was filled with a vague disquiet, and went out into the passage and through the front office as far as the street. But the whole town was dark and quiet, save for the sound that the wind makes in trees.

Therefore the thing was never spoken, and when the morrow came, the lieutenant told him some quite other thing.

XXIX

I remember the day of the picnic. I shall remember it till I die.

Seven of us went, my brother and his wife, and Pieter and Nella and the two children, and I myself; for Martha had gone to Rusfontein to watch the young dominee play. My brother sat in front with his son and grandson, and we packed him in with rugs, for he was still weak from the influenza; and from the heart too, but that he did not know. It was like packing a lion into a car, for he growled and threw his head about just as a lion does, and you do not know if it is pleased or will suddenly bite off your head.

Ah but the day was beautiful, with the sun shining as though it would shine for ever, and not a cloud in the blue bowl of the sky, and the grass country turning to the yellow of winter, and the grandfather talking to his grandson, and holding the small hand for pleasure, so that the fancy came to me that he was in truth talking to his son. For it is true of all good men, that life makes them more gentle in the end.

The two men left us at the Long Kloof, where the hills fall down in krantzes to the low country, and drove away to the pan.

There they drove the car quietly into the group of trees that grew there, and got out themselves quietly, with their glasses and the book, and a chair for my brother to sit on. There for an hour or more they stayed in hiding and watched the birds; it is not a thing that I understand, being myself but an ordinary lover of God's creatures, but if it grows into a madness, then you can watch for ever, and catch pneumonia like Japie Louw, and nearly die. But I know that they saw the grey heron and the *hamerkop,* and in the grass near the pan the *kiewietjies,* the ordinary one and the one the English call the blacksmith, because it makes a noise like a hammer on an anvil; also the secretary bird that walks delicate and solemn over the veld, looking for a snake; and on the pan itself the white-faced *bleshoender,* the yellowbill duck, and the little *duikertjie,* that seems to spend more time below than above.

Then suddenly my brother said in a low voice, look!

— Where, father?

— There.

Then because the son could not see, the father went and stood behind him, rested his arm on the son's shoulder, and pointed at the bird. But the son could see no bird, for he was again moved in some deep place within, and something welled up within him that if not mastered could have burst out of his throat and mouth, making him a girl or child. Therefore he could neither see nor speak.

Then his father said in excitement, look son, it runs.

But when his son made no answer, he said, can't you see?

And the son said in a low voice, I cannot see.

My brother said, it's the young men that are going blind, and he went and sat down in disgust, but really because he was weary.

The son moved away from him, and took out his glasses and wiped his eyes and was recovered; then he too said in excitement, Yes, I see.

My brother was up in a moment and he said, do you still think it's a *ruitertjie?* Have you ever seen a *ruitertjie* with so white a head?

— No, it's not a *ruitertjie.*

— What is it then?

— It's a phalarope. It must be a phalarope.

My brother sat down.

— Of course it's a phalarope, he said. The Englishman was wrong.

He chuckled.

— Sybrand will have to apologise, he said. He said I mustn't argue with such learned men.

He stood up again and had another long look through his glasses at the phalarope. Then he sighed and said, *Ja, nee,* we'd better get back for lunch.

Then they came back to us at the Long Kloof, and we sat there in the sun and ate our food. The father began to doze in his chair, and the son went off wandering into the Long Kloof, silent and grave, to walk among the ferns and the flowers, and the sounds of birds and waters, and the ghosts of childhood, and the memories of that innocence that can never come back again.

When it was time for our tea, I went to look for him, but could not find him. I climbed down over the rocks of the

krantz, and looked down at the low country far below, where
are the rocks and thorns and the hot red flowers. And while
I stood there I saw a movement below, and it was a man's
arms stretched out in front of him on a rock, not in the trees
of the kloof, but amongst the grass and stones of the krantz.
And I knew he was praying out of some distress. Therefore
I climbed down over the rocks, and came to him, and he
turned to watch me come.

— My child, my child, I said.

And he said to me with coldness, what do you want?

And I said to him, you were praying?

— Can't I pray?

— And I know what you were praying.

— You do, do you? That would please you, to know even
what your favourite prayed. Then you could still more possess him. How you would love to possess him. Then you
could say to his mother and father, his wife and his children,
it is I that possess him. For when he was a child, I desired
to possess him. And now he is a man, I still desire to possess
him. In God's name, have you no pride? Or must you be
taught again?

Then he turned and left me, and climbed out of the
rocks of the krantz, and went back to the others. And when
at last I returned, I do not know if he looked at me, for I
did not look at him.

So we drove back to Venterspan when the sun was almost
down, and the world was filled with beauty and terror. And
darkness came over the grass country, and over the continent
of Africa, and over man's home and the earth, and over us
all. And the sun went down, and never rose again.

XXX

Then the captain went on leave, and took his mother to Cape Town, a thousand miles away. And the new captain, Captain Jooste, came to take his place, and he was a red-faced and jolly man. And Sergeant Steyn returned from his holiday in Natal, and his daughter brought back with her the box with the small coloured shells.

And Pa Griesel died, suddenly. And his sons and daughters came and buried him, and took their mother away, so that the house stood sorrowful and empty. And the girl Stephanie was again without work. I went to Japie Grobler and said to him again, can't you get the girl away? And he said to me, under what law?

Then he tried to get her another job, but he had no great heart for it, for he said to me with petulance, the case is getting me down.

And one day the girl Stephanie was in the street, and saw the lieutenant. And because she was not a man and did not wear a hat, she put her hand up to her brow, with the palm facing outwards, to show her respect.

And she said, *Baas.*

And the lieutenant stopped, and though his heart was beating and his soul was troubled, there was no real cause for fear, for it is nothing that such a girl should speak in such a way to such a man. And the street was safe and sure, with the people all about, and the cars moving, and the sun shining.

— What is it, Stephanie?

— *Baas,* I am out of work.

And he could no longer say to her, why don't you go to Baas Grobler?

So he said to her, I have heard it.

— What shall I do, *baas?*

And while he considered it, having no answer, she said to him, if I make liquor, they will send me to prison, and take away my child.

— Have you money, he said.

— *Baas,* only a pound is left.

— I'll help you, he said. Then he said to her in a low voice, I can't give it to you here.

He looked at her unwillingly, and she looked at him with the great respect, with her open hand still held against her brow.

— I'll bring it tonight, he said.

— Thank you, *baas.*

So she left him and went on her way with a kind of walk that is not quite walking and not quite dancing, and it is a common thing, and has no great meaning in it, and it is nothing to see it in an open street, where all is safe and sure.

And the lieutenant went on, and Sergeant Steyn saluted

him stiffly there in the street. Now the world has eyes for a thousand things, but the prisoner for only one; and the prisoner of hate has one purpose and one alone, and that is to destroy what he hates. Therefore to the Sergeant, under the sun and in the open day, in a street safe and sure, with the cars and the people moving, came the one thought of the thousand, not as knowledge, but as a thing that might be so, so that all others would pass it by, except the one who has the hatred in his heart.

And that night the lieutenant took three pounds to the vacant ground and gave it to her, and did not break the law, but remembered his vow. And whether he did it out of his misery or what strange thing he did it out of, God knows, I do not know. But I cannot write down here that it was of God's mercy, nor of anything of God at all. Therefore I write, God knows, I do not know.

And the girl took her money humbly and with thanks, and he waited there as he had waited before, with fear. Then he came out of that place, and went through the dark streets to his house.

*   *   *   *   *

I have been to the great Falls in Rhodesia with my brother and his wife, and we have been on the great river, the Zambesi, in a boat. There are islands there, and quiet waters, and trees that hang down into them, and coloured birds calling and crying in the peace. Then the great river quickens and shudders, and goes streaming away before you green and foaming, and the boat quickens and shudders too, for you are drawing near to the great fall of smoke and thunder. And the captain turns the boat, so that it draws back from the brink, and you return to the islands and the safety and the peace.

And if we were to draw back from the brink and not go down to the great fall, then it was time to turn. But the captain was in Cape Town, a thousand miles away.

XXXI

And I could not go to Japie and say to him, in God's name Japie, you must do this and you must do that, before it is too late to turn, in God's name before it is too late to turn. Therefore I did not go.

And the other could not go to Japie and say, in God's name Japie, you must find a job, surely there must be a job, in God's name find a job. Therefore he did not go.

Therefore because there was no job, and because she was not sent away, she made more liquor, and was brought before the magistrate. And my sister-in-law and I were there, having been asked to be there by the magistrate. But the lieutenant was not there.

She did not stand there smiling and frowning, nor did she play with her fingers, but she stood there silent and watchful, till the magistrate asked her if she had anything to say.

— The magistrate said I must work, she said.

— Yes.

— So I got work with *Baas* Willemse.

— Yes.

— Then they heard I had been in prison, so they sent me away.

— Yes.

She turned and looked at Japie.

— Then the *baas* got work for me.

— Yes.

— And the *Oubaas* died.

— Yes.

— So I lost that work also.

— Yes.

Then she was silent, having no more to say.

— Then you did no work.

— No.

— You made more liquor.

— Yes.

— Therefore I must sentence you to two weeks in prison.

— What about the child?

— We will tell you about that when you come out of prison.

— I could get no work, she said.

Then when the magistrate made no answer, she said to him, I cannot lose the child.

And the magistrate said, fortunately or unfortunately, that will not be for you to say.

So she said to him again, I cannot lose the child.

Then they took her away, and I saw that she was like a tigress for the child, and it filled me with fear, though just of what I could not say. Then the magistrate sent a message to us, that he would like to see us in his office. I did not want to go, but my sister-in-law asked me to come with her, and I went. Japie was there also, and he did not tell the magistrate that he had no more heart for the case, but he told him that it was almost impossible to get a job for the girl in Venterspan.

Then I said, in a manner as though the idea had just come to me, could she not be sent away? And if the magistrate had not been there, Japie would have said to me, under what law? But the magistrate said, whether she is sent away or not, there is still the matter of the child. So he looked at my sister-in-law, because she was the President of the Women's Welfare Society, and I looked at her too, not because she was the President, but because I was afraid to speak, as a man is afraid to speak or move or turn when he knows he is in some danger, and does not know what it is, nor when or whence it will strike.

And my sister-in-law said, with her face full of love and care, I am sorry for the girl, but I tell myself I must think about the child.

And the magistrate said to her, I am sure you are right. This is the twelfth time that the girl has been sent to prison. When she comes out again, and if Mr. Grobler finds her a job, and if for some reason or other she loses the job, she will think again, as she obviously thinks now, that she has some kind of right to break the law. And how will the child grow up? Obviously to think that if he is not fed with a spoon, then he too has a right to break the law. If such a child is to be taken away, it should be done soon, for the longer he stays with his mother, the more likely is he to grow up into a *skelm*. I should say too that Mr. Grobler has already done more than he was obliged to do, for as far as I know, he is not obliged to find employment for such persons. Is that true, Mr. Grobler?

— That's true, *meneer*, said Japie.

— Still, said the magistrate to my sister-in-law, we have a Welfare Society, and it will always be my policy to try to follow their recommendations if I can honestly do so.

— I should like, said my sister-in-law, to take the case to our Committee.

So we took the case to our Committee, and they spoke about it for more than an hour; but I did not speak, being afraid to speak or move or turn. Nor did my sister-in-law speak, but sat herself like a magistrate, if a magistrate can be so gentle, and listened as a magistrate listens to all the people in the court, and then gives his sentence. So she gave her gentle sentence, that it was time to take away the child.

*   *   *   *   *

And it was about this time that I saw the envelope of stamps. My brother was sitting at the long table reading in the book, and when he heard me coming he put the envelope quickly between the pages, and sat there watchful and innocent, but I had seen.

I went to Kappie, and he was sitting in his little office, the one I always reproached him with. And I accused him and said, you've been selling my brother stamps.

He smiled and said to me, *mejuffrou*, how is it possible?

— It's not possible, I said. It just *is*. I've seen them.

— Did he show them to you, *mejuffrou*?

— Of course not, I said. He tried to hide them, but I saw them.

He smiled at me with much apology.

— It's a secret, he said.

— It's not a secret now, I said. Are they for the birthday?

He got up and shut the office door.

— They're for the birthday, he said.

And I sat there and thought to myself that no one would ever understand the world or its men and women.

— He came and sat there in your chair, said Kappie, and said, I have some private business. So I got up and shut the door, just as I shut it now. Then he looked at me angrily and said, I want to buy some stamps. I looked at him and said, stamps? He said to me, am I speaking badly? No, no, I said, I heard what you said. Then he said to me still angrily, what stamps would he like? So I sat and thought to myself, what stamps would the lieutenant like? Then I said to him, *meneer,* how much do you want to spend? So he said to me, perhaps you did not hear me, I said, what stamps would he like? So I said, *meneer,* will you wait? Then I went to my room and got one of my books, and I brought it back to him and showed him the block of the four triangular stamps, the same stamps I showed to the lieutenant on the morning his father was so angry. And the *Oubaas* said, how much are they, Kappie? And I told him, thirty-two pounds. He looked at them, and then at me, and he said to me, it's not a joke you're making? And I said to him, I can show you other stamps. So he said to me, he likes them, does he? I said, he thinks they're wonderful, *meneer.*

They must be wonderful, he said, why, I could buy the finest horse in the grass country for thirty-two pounds. Then he said, how much is a single stamp? Four pounds, I said. So, he said, who is going mad, Kappie, you or I? It's because

they're all together, I said. Kappie, he said, I'll sell you a
sheep for four pounds, and I'll sell you four for sixteen
pounds, and put them all together too. It's the way of the
stamps, I said. Why don't the farmers go in for stamps, he
said. Why do they waste their time on sheep?

— *Mejuffrou*, that is how he went on, said Kappie to me.
Ag, you know how he is.

— Go on, I said.

— So then he wrote the cheque for thirty-two pounds.
And he gave it to me and said, it's a robbery. I understand,
I said. Then he got up and put the envelope into his pocket,
and said to me, I'm glad you understand, for there's no one
else in South Africa could understand, except all other rob-
bers. So I walked out with him to the door, and at the door
he said, it's a robbery, but understand, it's a private robbery.
I don't want the whole grass country laughing behind my
back.

So I sat there and considered the strange story of the
stamps. And at another time one could have laughed over it,
and been filled with joy. But I did not laugh, nor was I filled
with joy.

— *Mejuffrou*, what's the trouble?

— Ag, I said.

— It's a deep trouble.

— Yes, I said.

Then Kappie told me how he felt like the man with the
puzzle that has a hundred pieces, and the picture is all but
complete, except for the six or seven pieces that will not fit.
Therefore it cannot be the picture at all. And it was in my
heart to tell him the one piece that I thought I knew, but I
was afraid. And it was in my heart to tell him of the hard

and bitter words that were spoken to me amongst the rocks of the krantz at Buitenverwagting, yet God forgive me, I pitied myself, and was ashamed that a man should think me a woman to whom such words could be spoken. So I was silent. And now as I write I am like a woman whose man is dead, because of some accident that was not foreseen, or because of some doctor that was not called, or because of some word that sounded like another; and she reproaches herself, and thinks that if for years she had not said, ah if we had a car, or if she had not said, let's go today not tomorrow, or if she had said, let's go by the lower road, perhaps her man would be alive again. And whether I could have saved him then, or whether if Kappie had known, he could have saved him then, or whether if the captain had been there, he could have saved him then, God knows, I do not know.

* * * * *

So the girl Stephanie returned from prison, and was called to the court, and was told that her child would be taken away, and would be given to some man and woman who had no child of their own, and were sober and law-abiding. So she left the court, but I did not see it then as I see it now, that she left it not like one on whom sentence is passed, but like one who passes it.

Not long after that the lieutenant was in the location, and one of the *klonkies* told him that the old woman Esther wished to speak to him. So he went to her house, but it was not the old woman Esther that wished to speak to him, it was the girl Stephanie.

And he said to her, hiding his fear, what do you want?

— They have taken my child, she said.

— I have heard it.

— I cannot be without my child, she said.

He looked at her, but he did not know what to say to her, for he feared her, and he feared her knowledge, and he feared her and her knowledge still more when she said, I told the *baas* I could not be without the child.

— I am not the magistrate, he said.

— It is not the magistrate, she said. It is the white women who have taken the child.

Then he knew what she would say.

— The *baas* knows these white women, she said.

— I know these white women, he said slowly, but they do not ask me what they must do.

— Then, she said, I must make another case.

And the words filled him with terror, so that he said in a voice not his own, what case? And she could see that he was troubled, so she said to him, with a lawyer.

So he stood there, afraid to stay and afraid to go away.

Then she said to him, this other case will also be for the child.

So the terror lifted, and he waited for her to speak again.

— The lawyer wants money, she said.

— How much money?

— Five pounds.

Then he said to her, I could give that money, but I am not rich, to go on giving money.

— It's the last money I shall ask, she said.

— I shall bring the money, he said.

— Tonight, she asked.

— Tomorrow night, he said.

Then she lifted her hand, and placed it palm outward

against her brow, and said to him humbly, I shall be glad for the money, *baas*. And it will be the last money that I ask.

So he went away, half with comfort, and half with fear, and walked back to the town, and vowed and prayed, and prayed and vowed, with the vow that he would keep the law, both of God and of Man, and with the prayer, *God wees my genadig, o Here Jesus wees my genadig*.

* * * * *

So I took the five pounds and went with fear to the vacant ground. And it was my purpose, made in prayer, to keep the law. And it was her purpose, for what reason I did not know, to break the law. And I carried out her purpose, and not my own which was made in prayer.

XXXII

Then he went home, filled with loathing of himself too deep to be uttered. When he got there Nella was in the dining-room, sitting by the fire. He did not go in to her, but called out, I'm going to have a bath, and she answered him, there's no need to make one of those tremendous fires, there's plenty of hot water in the pipes. Then he bathed himself from head to foot, trembling with the secret knowledge of the abject creature that was himself, that vowed and could not keep his vows, that was called to the high duty of the law and broke the law, that was moved in his soul by that which was holy and went reaching out for that which was vile, that was held in respect by men and was baser than them all. He thought he would go to Johannesburg, and see one of these psychiatrists, who might tell him some secret of salvation, for he had no more trust in his own power; nor any trust that he could find the secret of God's power. And he thought of the words that are written, ask and it shall be given, search and it shall be found, knock and it shall be opened, but they too held some secret that he could not find. And he thought of those other words that are written, no man shall be tempted beyond his power, but they too held some meaning that he could not find.

When he had cleansed his body he put on his pyjamas and dressing gown, and went and spoke to Nella. And this time because he was cleansed without even if unclean within, he put his head in at the door, and said to Nella, I'm going to work.

She said to him, I'll bring you some coffee.

He went into his study, and looked there amongst his learned books that told all the sins and weaknesses of men, hoping to find himself, though this he had already done, finding nothing. And he thought that perhaps he had expected to find it too easily, under some title ready-made, and that perhaps he should read more carefully.

Nella brought him his coffee and rusks, and said to him, what, another cigarette?

— It helps me to concentrate, he said.

— You'll have Hannes after you, she said.

And he smiled at her, not like a man who is master of himself, but one who is humble. And when she came to get the cup and plate, he would not let her carry them but carried them himself. And though it was not her habit, he was afraid that she might put her arm through his, and speak gentle words to him that he could not have borne.

Then she said, I'm tired, I'm going to bed, and held up her face to be kissed. And he kissed her on the brow, and did not open his lips; and sometimes when he did that, she said, what a kiss, and sometimes she did not, thinking nothing of it. And this night she did not, for which he was grateful.

So he went back to his books, but could not find himself there, at least not in any way that he could say, this is myself, this is myself beyond all doubt. So he read there of the misery of other men's lives, and the dark crimes and sins that they committed, and he did not know if they were sinning, or asking and seeking, and knocking at strange and terrible doors. And he found himself in a sad tormented company, and had pity for all twisted souls, and most for himself that found himself with them.

And all the day following he was filled with this new humility, and was full of helpfulness and small courtesies. And he would not allow Nella to do this and that, but did it for her, with some kind of sad gentleness, like a man who takes farewell of his friends, who know that he goes on some journey whose nature and end they do not understand. But this nature and end he understands, and is therefore silent because it is always in his mind, and is sad because of his knowledge, and is gentle as though it is his friends not he that stand in need of some compassion.

And I saw him in the street. He was standing outside the Royal talking to Abraham Kaplan, the brother of Kappie his friend. And Abraham Kaplan remembered only afterwards the courtesy and gentleness. For when his friends talked to the lieutenant, they knew only that he was talking to them, and they would not notice this or that; except Kappie, who being like myself set apart from the world, would notice this and that. While they were talking, Abraham Kaplan's daughter Rachel, the one that plays the violin, came out to go to school, out of their house that is next to the hotel, for Abraham Kaplan would not let his wife and daughter live in any hotel, not even a decent and quiet place like the Royal. And the lieutenant said to the girl, Rachel, how's the violin?

The girl blushed and made some answer, but Abraham Kaplan said with pride, it's going well, lieutenant.

And the lieutenant said to the girl, when are you going to play for us again?

For sometimes the girl played in some concert in Venterspan.

— My father doesn't like it, she said.

Abraham Kaplan shrugged his shoulders and put out his hands, and the lieutenant said to her, your father's right, your time will come. But don't worry; sometimes I hear you playing when I pass in the street.

Then he said to her, then I say just what your uncle says, that one day they will hear you play in far bigger places than this, not only here, but in other countries.

And the girl was filled with pleasure, and the father too, as any father is who hears such praise for his child; and proud too, because it was the lieutenant that gave the praise.

— One more year, said Abraham Kaplan and she goes away to study. And her mother goes too, so the old man will be left alone.

Then the lieutenant left them, and walked away down van Onselen Street. And they stood and watched him go, and spoke about him, as one speaks about a man who has given pleasure. But it was only afterwards that Abraham Kaplan remembered, that there was something in it not quite like other times.

And when I saw him in van Onselen Street, I turned at once into Kappie's store, for I remembered only the hard and bitter words that were spoken to me amongst the rocks of the krantz at Buitenverwagting, and was still ashamed that a man should think me a woman to whom such words could be spoken. And though I had seen him since, I could not face him alone and in an open street.

But he came after me into the store, where I stood at the counter talking to Kappie. He put his arm through mine, and put his hand on my arm above the wrist, and held it tightly, and talked to Kappie, and with his hand asked my forgiveness. So with my arm I pressed his own against me, and talked to Kappie, and with my arm forgave him. And he left us there.

Then he went to the Police Station, and took the inspection with Sergeant Steyn, and then went to his office. And it was the end of June, and pay day, and the young boy Vorster brought him another pound, and said to him, lieutenant, that leaves eighteen pounds. And the lieutenant said, I told you you were clever.

After his work he went home again, and again was full of helpfulness. With the children he was not loud or rough, nor dark and silent, but stood over them quietly when they were in the bath, and afterwards dried them with love and care, and took them to the room and heard their prayers. After dinner they sat before the fire, his wife busy with some work, and he with a book, not of twisted souls, but some sweeter book. He feared that she might speak to him or touch him, and did not know what he would say or do. And he would have suffered it, but she neither spoke nor touched him, and when she said she would go to bed, he rose and kissed her, but this time on her lips, for he felt cleaner.

Then he sat alone by the fire, and the thought, the hope, came to him that this strange mood of humility and gentleness might be some turning point, and that this perhaps might be the finding of that which was sought, and the opening of the door that was knocked on. So with some kind of peace he went to his bed.

Ag, what things are moods, that come and go like the wind that blows where it lists. For a man can be happy and free, and be cast down by a word. And a woman can be in the depths of misery, and be lifted up by an asking for forgiveness. So one goes from joy to dejection, and hurt to exaltation, and certainty to doubt, as when with some summer storm the whole world is dark and sombre, till suddenly the sun breaks through, almost at its setting, and bathes tree and grass and hill in green and yellow light, the like of which, as the English say, was never seen on land or sea.

XXXIII

And the next day the quiet and humble mood persisted, until the young dominee telephoned, and said he had had a letter from Hippo du Toit, who as everyone knows, is the famous rugby coach at Stellenbosch, and the greatest in the country.

— Pieter, he thinks you're a certainty.

— Does he? And what about yourself?

— Well, he doesn't feel too badly about that either.

— Good for you.

— Wouldn't that be good, Pieter?

— It would be good.

— Two Springboks from Venterspan, Pieter. Have they had one before?

— No, never.

The young dominee sat at the other end of the telephone, contemplating the future with bliss. Then he said, Pieter.

— Yes.

— I think I'm beginning to understand the old man.

— Are you?

— I think so. I think I'm beginning. Only beginning, you understand.

— I understand. What's this I hear about Dominee Stander?

— What did you hear?

— I heard he was angry with you.

— What for, Pieter?

— For neglecting your work.

— Ag, you're joking, Pieter.

— All right, I'm joking. How's my sister?

And the young dominee sat again, and contemplated both present and future with bliss.

— Pieter, I can't tell you over the telephone.

— Why not?

— Ag, it wouldn't seem right. I'll tell you this afternoon at the practice.

Then Japie came in, with his case full of papers.

— Old brother, he said, I think I can get the girl Stephanie a job.

And the lieutenant did not speak, but looked at his friend watchfully.

— Abraham Kaplan says he's willing to give her a chance at the hotel.

And the lieutenant forced himself to speak, and said, it's too late.

— Now, listen, old brother, you're not the only one that has the black nation on his heart. I suggested to the magistrate that we might send the child away temporarily, and if the girl proves herself, we might let her have it back.

— What did he say?

— He said he's willing to consider it.

And the lieutenant said to his friend humbly, you're a good chap, Japie.

— Of course I'm a good chap. You know it, everyone in Venterspan knows it, but the trouble is, do they know it in Pretoria?

He put his arms on the table and spoke confidentially.

— If I'm to get married, he said, I must earn some more money, for the truth is, old brother, this old Empire builder hasn't got a penny.

— So you're going to get married.

— Slowly now, slowly, old brother. I said *if* I'm to get married.

— So you haven't asked her yet?

Japie blushed.

— To tell you the truth, old brother, I have, and I haven't. I told her I'm not the marrying sort, but I have an idea I might change into the marrying sort. I couldn't have put it clearer, could I?

The lieutenant laughed.

— Japie, you're wonderful.

— *Ag*, I know I'm wonderful. The truth is, old brother, I'm almost willing, *almost* willing, you understand, to marry this girl and her father, and the King and Queen and the whole British Empire.

Then he took his arms off the table and looked at the floor.

— *Ag*, it's a state, he said. Old brother, I must go.

So the lieutenant went home to his lunch light-hearted and gay, and ate his lunch with Nella in the garden, with the birds and the sun. And he went back to his work light-heartedly, and as he was turning into the Police Station, he saw two men come out of Pretorius Street, the street that goes to the black people's location, the street with the blue-gum trees and the vacant ground. And one was Captain Jooste, and the other was his own captain that should have been in Cape Town, a thousand miles away.

XXXIV

Therefore he went to his room and closed the door, and sat there alone with the fear and the terror. And while he was sitting there, Sergeant Fourie came to him and said, Captain Jooste wants to see you, lieutenant.

Therefore he went to the captain's office, and knocked and went in, but no Captain Jooste was there, only his own captain. And his own captain looked more than ever grave and austere.

— Shut the door, van Vlaanderen. And sit down.

Therefore he sat down.

— I received an urgent call in Cape Town last night from Captain Jooste. So I flew up to Johannesburg this morning, and came down at once by car. You can see it was a most serious thing.

— Yes, sir.

— It's a charge, van Vlaanderen, a charge against you under Act 5 of 1927.

— Act 5?

And the captain did not look up, but at the papers, and he said in a low voice, yes, the Immorality Act.

And when the lieutenant did not speak, he said, the allegation is that on the night of Monday last you went to the vacant ground in Pretorius Street, and committed an offence under the Act.

And the lieutenant said, how is it possible?

— Is it true, van Vlaanderen?

— No, sir.

— I hope, and I pray too, that it isn't true, said the captain.

— It isn't true, sir.

— You are prepared to give every assistance, van Vlaanderen, so that the charge can be investigated?

— Yes, sir.

— What kind of jacket do you wear, van Vlaanderen, when you're off duty? How many jackets have you?

— Only one, sir. The rest are blazers.

— And flannels? How many pairs have you?

— Two, sir.

— One new, and one old?

— Yes, sir.

— And shoes?

— Three pairs, sir.

— What kind of shoes?

— One black pair, sir, and two brown pairs.

— The black pair for Sundays?

— Yes, sir.

— And the brown pairs? One old, and one new?

— Yes, sir.

— Would Mrs. van Vlaanderen think it strange if you

sent for your jacket, and the older pair of flannels, and the older pair of brown shoes?

— I don't think so, sir.

The captain pushed over pencil and paper to the lieutenant.

— Ask her to send them in a suitcase, van Vlaanderen. No, wait. Before you ask her, tell me again, can this charge possibly be true?

— No, sir.

— Then write the note, van Vlaanderen.

When the note was written, the captain took it, and he said to the lieutenant, give me your revolver. Therefore the lieutenant gave the captain his revolver. Then the captain went out and shut the door, and left the lieutenant for twenty minutes with the fear and the terror, wondering what terrible secret there could be in the jacket and flannels and shoes.

Then the two captains came back with the suitcase, in which were the jacket and flannels and shoes. His own captain put a drawing on the table in front of the lieutenant and said to him, that is the print of a rubber-soled shoe, taken in the vacant ground. Is it your own?

— No, sir.

— You have never been into this vacant ground?

— No, sir.

Then the captain opened the case, and took out the pair of shoes.

— I should tell you, van Vlaanderen, that a piece of earth was recently dug over in the vacant ground. A small piece of earth about two foot square. The print was made on the piece of earth.

Then the two captains compared the sole of the shoes with the drawing of the print, but the pattern was not the same.

— Would you take out the jacket, van Vlaanderen?

So the lieutenant took out the jacket.

— Is there anything in the left-hand pocket of the jacket, van Vlaanderen?

And the lieutenant felt with fear in the pocket, but found nothing.

— Nothing, sir.

— Look again, van Vlaanderen. It's a small object.

So the lieutenant felt again, and brought out from the pocket one of those small coloured shells that lie on the Natal beaches under the sun.

— The charge states, van Vlaaderen, that the girl called Stephanie put such a shell in your pocket on the night of Monday last, when you were standing in the vacant ground. Is that true, van Vlaanderen?

— It cannot be true, sir.

Then his own captain made a sign to Captain Jooste, and he went out and returned with Sergeant Steyn.

— Sergeant, where did you get this shell?

And the sergeant held out a box, and said, from this box, captain.

— And the box?

— My daughter brought it back, captain, with shells that she collected on the beach.

And the captain said to the sergeant coldly, and you gave one of these shells to the girl Stephanie?

— Yes, captain.

— With the instructions to put it into the left-hand pocket of a jacket that a man was wearing?

— Yes, captain.

And the lieutenant said, I had that jacket, sir, when I had my own leave in Natal.

— At the coast?

— Yes, sir.

— Then the captain said to the sergeant coldly, is there anything special about this shell?

— Yes, captain. It is filled with candle grease.

So the captain showed the shell to the lieutenant, and it was filled with candle grease.

— One thing more, sergeant. Where were you on the night of Monday last?

— In Pretorius Street, captain.

— And you saw a man come down Pretorius Street, and go into the vacant ground?

— Yes, sir.

— And you recognised him?

— Yes, sir.

— Who was it?

And the sergeant drew himself up stiff and straight, and showed no sign of joy or hate, and he said, it was Lieutenant van Vlaanderen, captain.

— And one thing more, sergeant.

— Yes, captain.

— It was you yourself who prepared the earth in the vacant ground?

And the sergeant said, with no sign of joy or hate or shame or grief, yes, captain.

— Then you may go.

Then the captain put five pound-notes on the table, and he said to the lieutenant, the girl states further that you gave her this money at this place and time.

But the lieutenant made no answer.

— And she states further that you committed an offence under the Act.

And still the lieutenant made no answer.

So the captain said to him, do you still deny it?

And the lieutenant stood up, and looked at the two captains out of his strained and desperate eyes. And he said, I can see that I am guilty.

His own captain said gently, what do you mean, you can see that you are guilty?

And the lieutenant said, like a child, I can see that everything is against me.

And the captain said gently, what do you mean, van Vlaanderen? Are you guilty, or not guilty?

— I am not guilty.

Then Captain Jooste, the red-faced and jolly captain, went out and shut the door.

— You're sure you are not guilty?

— I'm sure I am not guilty.

— Then, said the captain gravely, will you write another note to your wife, and ask her to send the other pair of shoes?

Then the lieutenant sat down, and put his head on his arms, and sobbed like any child. And the captain telephoned to Captain Jooste, and told him to keep everyone away from that place; and then he sat down in his chair opposite the lieutenant, and he said to him when he could, why didn't you tell me all this?

And the lieutenant lifted his head and said with grief, and that longing that comes in grief to return to some day that never will come again, I tried to tell you, I tried to tell you.

And the captain said sorrowfully, and I told you it could wait till tomorrow.

— Yes.

— My God, my God.

Then the lieutenant told him of the vows and the penitences, and the prayers in season and out, and the sitting amongst the oxen that were holy and obedient beasts, and the days of terror, and of his love for his wife and his children, and for his gentle mother, and of the mad sickness and the loathing, and of the great relief from terror and his laughter and his joy, and of the books of the twisted and tormented men, and of his decisions to speak, to Kappie and the captain himself or some psychiatrist, and of the hard and bitter words that he spoke to me at Buitenverwagting. And when this tale of past and present was done, he would have spoken of the future, but he drew back from it, unable to look it in the face, for the whole world was heaving and shaking, and God knew what terror and grief and anger was yet to come, in the hearts of men and women, in streets and houses and churches and bars and rooms. Therefore he put his head on his arms, and sobbed like any child.

And the captain went to him, and put his hand on his shoulder and said to him, there are terrible things to come, but I'll stand by you, by all of you, and do what I can do.

Then he went for Captain Jooste and asked him if he would sit with the lieutenant. So Captain Jooste sat with the lieutenant, while the captain went to do the duties that must still be done.

But he stopped as he went out of the Police Station, and he said to Sergeant Steyn who was alone, may God forgive you for an evil deed.

For once a charge is made, a charge is made; and once a thing is written down, it will not be unwritten. And a word can be written down that will destroy a man and his house and his kindred, and there is no power of God or Man or State, nor any Angel, nor anything present or to come, nor any height, nor any depth, nor any other creature that can save them, when once the word is written down.

XXXV

And while the captain was walking along van Onselen Street to our house, my brother was telling Sybrand Wessels and my sister-in-law and me the story of old Theunis Burger and his failing eyesight. For Theunis Burger sent for the doctor and told him he was going blind.

And the doctor said to Theunis, *meneer,* can you see the mountains? And Theunis looked in the direction of the mountains, and shook his head sorrowfully and said, no, I cannot see the mountains. So the doctor pointed and said, *meneer,* can you see those trees, and Theunis again shook his head sorrowfully and said, no, I cannot see any trees. Then the doctor shook his head also and said, that's bad, *meneer;* so he pointed nearer at hand and said, *meneer,* can you see those cows? And Theunis looked and said again sorrowfully, no, I cannot see any cows. Then the doctor was also sorrowful, and pointed again and asked earnestly, *meneer,* are you sure you cannot see the cows? So Theunis looked more carefully than ever, even shading his eyes, and saying with the greatest sorrow of all, no, I cannot see any cows, but I can see some oxen.

And Sybrand snorted and blew his nose, and behaved more like a girl than a man who would never be sixty again. And my sister-in-law and I laughed too, not at the story, for we had heard it before, but at the way my brother told it. For you could see Theunis Burger and his mischief before your very eyes.

That was the last such story told in our house, for the captain knocked at the door. I opened it, and when I saw how grave was the captain's face, I did not say to him, I thought you were in Cape Town, I said only, *goeie middag,* captain, and let him in. But my brother said, I thought you were in Cape Town. The captain said, I was in Cape Town, but an urgent matter brought me back again. Then he looked round gravely at us all, and especially at Sybrand Wessels, and said to my brother, *meneer,* I have a very private matter to discuss with you. So Sybrand Wessels left us.

Then the captain looked at my sister-in-law and me, and said again to my brother, it is a very private matter. And my sister-in-law got up, and she and I would have gone out, but I could see that my brother did not want to be left alone with this very private matter, for he said to the captain, as though he had some foreknowledge, does it concern us all? The captain said gravely, it concerns you all, but he looked again at us two women, so that we were again ready to go, had not my brother said finally, then tell us all. And the captain looked unwilling, but he was no doubt thinking to himself, *sooner or later,* so he said, as you wish, *meneer.*

Then my sister-in-law and I sat down, and my brother asked the captain to sit down also, but he said that he would tand.

— It is a very painful duty I have to perform, he said.

And my brother said in a low voice, perform it then.

— I was in Cape Town, said the captain, when Captain Jooste telephoned me, and asked me to return at once, on a most urgent matter.

— What is the urgent matter?

— The urgent matter, said the captain, is that a charge has been laid against your son, Lieutenant van Vlaanderen, that on Monday night of this week he committed an offence under the Immorality Act of 1927.

And my brother said unbelieving, the Immorality Act?

— Yes.

And my brother said nothing. He was sitting with his arms stretched out before him on the table, as he has them out when the Book is between them, only no Book was between them now. He did not look at us nor at the captain but straight before him. And I did not look at my sister-in-law, but I could see her out of the corner of my eye, and she sat without moving. And I sat without moving also, thinking to myself, thinking to myself, but what does it matter what I thought to myself, except that I knew that the whole house was destroyed, because I had not hammered and hammered on the door, and cried out, not ceasing. And the captain did not move either, but stood there gravely in front of us all.

Then my brother said, is the charge true?

— I fear it is true, said the captain.

Then my brother said, are you sure it is true?

Then the captain said, that is a matter for a court.

But my brother persisted, are you yourself sure?

And the captain said, he has confessed to me.

After that all was silence, except that my brother's breathing could be heard by us all, like the breathing of some creature in pain. But he did not look at us, he stared in front of him; and my sister-in-law looked down at her hands; and the captain stood like a soldier in front of us all.

Then the sound of my brother's breathing ceased, and he said to me, Sophie, the Book. So I brought him the Book, and put it between his arms, and wondered where he would read; but he did not read at all, he opened it at the beginning where are all the names of the van Vlaanderens, for more than a hundred and fifty years.

Then he said to me, Sophie, the pen and the ink.

So he took the pen and the ink, and he crossed out the name of Pieter van Vlaanderen from the Book, not once but many times, not with any anger or grief that could be seen, nor with any words.

Then he said to the captain, is there anything more?

Now whether the captain had anything more or not I could not say, but he had seen the crossing out of the name from the Book, and he went to my sister-in-law and took her hands, which she had in her lap not moving, and he said to her, you have my help in anything that you need.

And my brother said, no one will ask help from this house.

The captain looked at him, and then again at my sister-in-law, and he said to her, I'll stand by the boy. Then he looked again at my brother and said to him, I'll stand by the boy.

And my brother said, you will do what you wish, and then he looked at the captain, waiting for him to go. So the captain left us.

I followed the captain, and my brother said to me, lock the door and bolt it, and bring me the key.

I brought him the key, and he said to us, the door shall not be opened again.

Then he said to me, telephone to Buitenverwagting and tell Frans to come at once, alone.

I went to the telephone, and left husband and wife together, and they sat there neither moving nor speaking. When I came back I said, he is coming at once.

— You will take the book, he said, and the pipe, and everything that the man ever gave to me, and every likeness of him, and everything in this house that has anything to do with him, and you will burn and destroy them all. And bring me paper to write.

So while I collected together the pipe, and the book of birds, and every likeness of the man, and everything that had ever anything to do with him, he sat and wrote; he wrote to Dominee Stander, and to the Nationalist Party, and to the Farmers' Society, and to every other thing to which he belonged, and gave up all his offices and honours. And while I did the collecting and he did the writing, which took upwards of the hour, the mother of the man, of the child who had first opened the womb, sat with her hands in her lap, not moving, not speaking.

And then Frans came, and knocked at the door which would never be opened, and I told him to come in by the door at the side of the house. My brother pointed him to the Book, and said you know whose name was there. And Frans said, yes, father, and stood there with his heart beating and his face white, because he knew that some terrible thing had befallen us. Then my brother told him what the man had done, and that his name must never again be spoken in that house, nor any likeness of him be seen there, nor any thing that had been his or had to do with him. Then he ordered Frans to go at once, and to take the man's wife and his children at once to Buitenverwagting, and to give them the old house where he and my sister-in-law had lived when they were married; and he told Frans to let Nella's father and mother know what terrible fate had befallen their house also, and also to let his own sisters know at once.

Then he told me to telephone to the lawyer de Villiers, and tell him to come at once, and after that to tell the telephone people to come and take away the telephone that very day. Then the lawyer de Villiers came, and I had to bring him in by the door at the side of the house; and they changed the will, giving Frans the portion of the elder son, and giving the second portion to Nella and her children, on condition that neither she nor they ever again had any commerce with the man.

When Frans and the lawyer de Villiers had gone, my brother ordered me to sit down, and though it was still day, he took the Book and read the words of the Hundred and Ninth Psalm, which are the most terrible words that man has ever written, and should not be in any holy book. For it is written there

When he shall be judged, let him be condemned; and let his prayer become sin.

Let his days be few; and let another take his office.

Let his children be fatherless, and his wife a widow.

Let his children be continually vagabonds, and beg; and let them seek their bread also out of their desolate places.

Let the extortioner catch all that he hath; and let the strangers spoil his labour.

Let there be none to extend mercy unto him; neither let there be any to favour his fatherless children.

Let his posterity be cut off; and in the generation following let their name be blotted out.

Let the iniquity of his fathers be remembered with the Lord; and let not the sin of his mother be blotted out.

Let them be before the Lord continually, that he may cut off the memory of them from the earth.

Because that he remembered not to show mercy, but persecuted the poor and needy man, that he might even slay the broken in heart.

When my brother had finished reading, he suddenly bowed himself over the Book, and my sister-in-law moved at last, and lifted her head to look at him. Perhaps he heard it, and it moved him in some deep place within, for he said in a voice of agony, I shall not pray. She stood up and went to him, and put her arm on his shoulder, nothing more; and his head bowed still further over the Book, till his face almost rested upon it. He stayed there for a minute maybe, till he had mastered himself; then he raised his head and closed the Book, and stood up from his chair, turning away from us, and making for the stairs to his room. When he had climbed two or three, she followed him, and said, Jakob, I must go to him. He stopped, and without turning he said to her, you must do what you wish, but if you once go out of this house, you shall not enter it again.

Then she looked at me, and I said to him, I will go then.

— You are leaving us, he asked.

— If it must be, I said.

— If you go out, he said, it must be.

— Then it must be, I said.

Now I had lived in my brother's house these thirty years, which is not something so easily brought to an end; therefore he turned.

— Then I will say farewell to you, he said, and he bowed his head to me.

— I wish you well, he said.

Then he waited a moment, two moments, for an answer, but the only answer that came to my mind was *I wish you well also*, but how could I say such a thing? So without my answer he turned and went up the stairs, and my sister-in-law watched him from the stairs, and I from the room below, till we heard the sound of his closing door.

Then she came down the stairs to me, and we embraced, but not weeping.

At last she said, did you burn them all?

— Not all.

— What did you keep?

— A photograph, I said.

— Give it to me, she said.

So we went to my room, and I took the photograph from under my pillow, and gave it to her; and it was one of which she was most fond, of the soldier away at the war, and she looked at it with grief and love.

— What did you keep for yourself, she said.

So fearing, I took out the book of the birds, and she cried out for what might have been, and for the memory of the

night the book was given, and for sorrow of the thought of
the deep things of fathers and sons and childhood, that no
man understands. And she told me how from the years of
childhood she had feared for him, and had known that he
was hiding away, in some deep place within, things that no
man might safely conceal; and how, not knowing what they
might be, she had prayed ceaselessly that they might be removed. Yet now she knew, her love was multiplied.

And she remembered, when he had been so happy in
love, that her hope had been renewed; but soon she had
known that even then he had not revealed himself, so that
the girl Nella had married a stranger, whom the oldest and
wisest could neither help nor understand. And she said to
me, she has no blame, let the whole world know it.

Then she said to herself, dear child, unhappy child.

Then she said to me, who will dare to judge her? Neither
you nor I. For God is both Lover and Judge of men, and it
is His commandment that we join Him in loving, but to
judge we are forbidden. You will say both to my son and to
my daughter that my love is multiplied, and although I am
shut off from them by the door of a house, all the doors of
my heart are open; I will remember them by day and by
night, till I am permitted to go to my rest. But this love that
I may not show, you will show for me.

And I could not answer her, being rebuked and shamed;
and afraid also, never having heard such words from her
before.

— And you will say to my son, she said, that though he
may suffer under the law, there is no law that can cut him
off from our love, nor from the love of his friends. His life

is God's, and mine and yours, and his wife's and children's,
and all his friends'; and he will therefore cherish it and not
despair.

— Now go, she said, and quickly.

She kissed me and said, I am going to my husband.

So I went and packed some clothes, and when I was
done I went out, but I did not dare to go quickly as she had
bidden me, for the darkness of the street was not yet dark
enough. And I did not dare to go back into the house, partly
because it was now forbidden, and partly because I did not
wish to face my sister-in-law, who would have gone in any
dark or light. And because I did not wish to face the girl
Martha when she came home, I went and sat in the garden;
and while I was sitting there, she came, and the young
dominee with her, and knocked on the door which would
not be opened, and I heard my sister-in-law's voice from the
house, low and quiet, telling them to go to the other door,
and they passed near to me, and even in that light I could
see that they knew. Therefore it was known, and would go
like fire from every house to every house, and from every
farm to every farm in the grass country, and down with
kloof and precipice to the hot world of rock and flower, and
to every kraal and hut of Maduna's people, and over the
telephone wires and the telegraph wires, into every town
and city, and into the newspapers, and into the homes of
soldiers who had fought in the war, and into the offices of
Pretoria, and even into the great rugby fields where tens of
thousands came to see the game. Therefore I waited till the
darkness was complete.

Then I ventured out into the street with the three pools
of light, and when I came near to the Royal Hotel I crossed

over into the dark, and so came to the Police Station, and went to the captain's office, and said, where is he?

— He's just gone home, he said.

— There's no one there, I said. My brother had them taken away.

— Come at once, he said.

As we hurried into the street, he said to me anxiously, he wanted to tell her himself, he was desperate to tell her himself. And in thirty minutes I was to go there myself.

— Did you take the guns?

— All the guns and his revolver.

— And his own revolver? His private revolver?

— I didn't know he had one. Can you go faster?

— I can run, I said.

XXXVI

For as soon as it was dark, Sergeant Fourie had taken the ex-lieutenant to his house. And the ex-lieutenant had shown him the guns, but himself stood listening, for there was no sound in the house, of woman, or of children playing in the bath. Then the sergeant went, and the boy Johannes came out of the kitchen, all smiles and cheerfulness; and because the boy was smiling and cheerful, the man was able to say to him, almost as though it were nothing, who fetched the mistress and the children? And the boy said, *Baas* Frans came with the car. And the man said carelessly, is there a letter? And the boy said, there is a letter.

The boy went to the kitchen and came back with the letter, which was heavy and addressed to P. van Vlaanderen. He tore it open, and it was full of paper money, with a note on which was written, *Hiermee jou agtien pond, J. Vorster,* which is, *Herewith your eighteen pounds.* But the English is not the same as the Afrikaans, for the word *jou* when used in this way, is a word of supreme contempt.

Then he saw it was beyond all reason, and he went to

the bedroom and took out the revolver from the cupboard where it was kept, and put his big coat over his uniform, and went out into the darkness of the town.

Therefore when the captain and I came, he was already gone. But we saw the money and the letter, and though we did not understand about the money, we knew it was a letter of supreme contempt. I went to the bedroom and looked round it helpless, not knowing where the thing was kept, and therefore not knowing if it were gone. I went running to the captain and said to him, where shall we go?

— God knows, he said. But we can try.

Therefore we went hurrying through the town, to Pretorius Street, where the stinking *kakiebos* grows on the vacant ground.

Now Kappie came also hurrying to the house, when he heard that his friend was there alone. And he too saw the money and the letter of supreme contempt. Therefore he went out at once, but he did not go to the vacant ground, but to Slabbert's Field; and there on the lowest row of seats he saw his friend in the dark, sitting with his hands held together on his knees, and his head bowed into his breast. And Kappie came down quietly over the rows of seats, till he was standing two or three rows behind him.

Then he said, lieutenant.

And the man did not turn, but he said at once, who are you?

— Kappie, lieutenant. Lieutenant, in God's name, and in the name of your Lord Jesus Christ, put down that revolver.

And the man said, I am not a lieutenant.

So Kappie said, Pieter, in God's name, put it down.

Then he heard the revolver fall from his friend's hands, and he came down over the rows of seats, and sat down beside him, and put his arm about him, not round the shoulders, for he could not, being so small a man. And he spoke to him there, as one speaks to a child, as a woman speaks, as most men would fear to speak in the presence of any other person, about friends and courage, and about no one deserving to suffer for ever, and about a plan for man and wife and children to go to some new country, where they could forget the terror and suffering.

— My wife and children, Kappie? They've gone already.

Then Kappie had to speak to him again, about panic and danger, and how one turned to flee, and could not then remember past love and mercies. He spoke as a woman speaks to her child when sobbing is past, one questioning and questioning, the other answering and comforting, so that the present is secure and warm, and it seems almost that the future will not come.

Then Kappie stood up, and picked up the revolver.

— Pieter, let us go home.

— Kappie.

— Yes?

— Did you know?

— I knew there was something, but I didn't know what it was.

— I tried to tell you, Kappie.

And Kappie stood there remembering, and out of the silence of Slabbert's Field came suddenly, rising and falling in the dark, the music of the great Concerto, matching the sorrow of this night and the world, so loud and clear he wondered that the other did not hear.

Yet perhaps he heard, for he said, I went there to tell you.

And together they listened to the music of that time, when a man went to speak and did not speak, not even a word of the coldness and beauty of the winter's night, when a man pursued by mortal danger drew back from the very edge of his salvation, and was destroyed.

And the music died away, and Slabbert's Field was a field again, cold and dark, and one knew that the future must come.

So in silence they walked back to the town, and passed us in the dark; and when they had gone into the house, the captain and I came slowly after.

XXXVII

But though the captain and I followed, we did not go into the room, but stood at the door; for he was saying that he was cleansed, once and for ever, and that this blow that had struck him down had cleansed him for ever, but why must a man be struck down to be cleansed, and why could not the man who had struck him down have warned him, for by this very warning he would have been cleansed for ever, and why could not God have warned him, and why must God strike him down so utterly, and why must the innocent also be struck down, and why and why and why?

So I knew that he had been destroyed. For he was like a man who had lived famous by some legend, that underneath his clothes he was not like other men, but had the parts of a god; but some enemy had made him drunken, and stripped him and left him in the streets for men's derision. And the thought came to me, sudden and shocking, that the broken and the contrite heart is something far more terrible than penitence. Ah, why must we armour ourselves? Oh that we had some deeper love and knowledge, that no child would ever again be hurt.

— And Kappie, my mother?

And Kappie said, we must wait for your aunt.

Therefore I went in and said, your mother sends her love. And Kappie went out, and the boy put his arms about me, and pressed his head into my breasts, and was as he had been as a child, before the time he humbled me.

And whether because of this, or whether because of something other, but he ceased to torment himself, and began to speak, as one speaks after the first agony of bereavement is past, as one might stand up and say, *would you like to see his picture as a child?*

So now he said to me, do you understand it all?

— Something, I said. Not all.

He stood up and went into his study, and brought back a leather bag which must have been in the chimney, for it was black with soot. Out of it he took a paper parcel, which he opened out on to the floor, and out of the parcel a big envelope. His hands were sooty, and he said to me earnestly and like a boy, open it, Tante, it's clean.

I took it up and on it was written

> In the event of my death to be given
> unopened to
>   Matthew Kaplan
>   Southern Transvaal Trading Store
>   Venterspan.
> P. van Vlaanderen.

I opened it and in it was a thick black book, such as the older children use at school.

— It's all there, he said, I wrote it all down.

— Is this for Nella, I said.

— For Nella, he said, and if she wishes, for my mother and yourself.

Then we talked no more, and the captain and Kappie came in when they heard us silent.

Kappie said, Pieter, can I sleep here tonight?

So I, who had wished to sleep there myself, was humble and took up my case, and was ready to go with the captain.

In the street he said to me, did you mean to sleep there?

— Yes.

Then he would have taken me to my brother's house, but I told him that I was forbidden to return, and would go to the hotel.

— You'll go to no hotel, he said. You'll come to my mother's house.

After that he spoke no more, till we reached the gate of the house; then he stopped, and said to me in a strange and trembling voice, an offender must be punished, *mejuffrou*, I don't argue about that. But to punish and not to restore, that is the greatest of all offences.

— Is that the sin against the Holy Ghost, I said.

— I don't know, he said, but I hope not, for I once committed it. But I am resolved never again to commit it.

And I dared to say to him, was that your son?

— Yes, he said. Yes, it was my son.

He opened the gate.

— Everything in this house is yours, *mejuffrou*.

And I answered him lightly, I shan't take it all.

— *Mejuffrou*, he said to me gravely, you're a lovely woman.

But to that I made no answer, it being the first time that such a thing was ever said to me.

When we went into the house, Nella's father was waiting for us, the tall and fierce old man, with the face like that of an eagle, and the blue and piercing eyes. To him the captain told the story of all, and when he had finished, the fierce old man struck the arm of his chair and said, I would shoot him like a dog.

Then because no one spoke, he said to the captain, wouldn't you?

And the captain said, No.

— You wouldn't?

— No.

— But he has offended against the race.

Then the captain said trembling, *Meneer,* as a policeman I know an offence against the law, and as a Christian I know an offence against God; but I do not know an offence against the race.

So the old man turned to me and said, *Mevrou.* . . .

— *Mejuffrou,* I said.

Then he recognised me at last, for all his piercing eyes, and said, *mejuffrou,* I am sorry. . . .

— *Meneer,* said the captain, if man takes unto himself God's right to punish, then he must also take upon himself God's promise to restore. If we . . .

— You are an Englishman, said Nella's father, fiercely but without offence. You do not understand these things.

— I am not an Englishman, I said, but I understand them.

The old man said, it will not help to stay any longer, and with a brief *goeie nag,* he went.

The captain said to me, when are you going to take the book?

When I did not answer immediately, he said, I hope you will take it soon.

I said, out of some foolishness, will that help?

He said quietly, if she doesn't come back, nothing will help at all. You surely don't think, *mejuffrou*, that some other woman could save him? And if you are thinking, *she couldn't help before*, don't you see this is quite another man?

— I'm sorry, I said. I didn't mean to say it.

— I'm not thinking only of him, he said, but of her also. There's a hard law, *mejuffrou*, that when a deep injury is done to us, we never recover until we forgive.

— I'll take the book, I said. *Ag*, but I'm afraid.

XXXVIII

So we were all struck down. Because he would not tell one man, therefore the whole world knew. His father shut the door of his house, and his brother would not leave the shelter of Buitenverwagting, and his married sisters hoped that none would remember their unmarried names. His young sister Martha had given back her ring, and the young dominee did not know whether to take it or refuse; nor did the old dominee know how to counsel him, being torn between his love for the man and his love for the Church, that must be beyond reproach, and not a cause of stumbling. For I said to the old dominee, as the Lord is the Lord of Love, so must His Church be the Church of Love, else will He destroy it. And he replied, *mejuffrou*, it is His to destroy, not yours or mine.

But it was not left to the young dominee to decide, for the girl herself said that never again would she leave the house, not because of her father's will, but of her own. Nor did she cling to her lover with tears and despair, but would not let him even touch her. Therefore I write here that her

brother's offence destroyed her also. Life struck her across
the face, and brought her from a young girl's dreaming into
a hard and angry world, where love seemed foolishness.
And some of its hardness entered into her also, so that she
could see her lover before her unhappy and distraught, and
not be moved to touch and comfort him.

— So you're going, I said to him.

— Tante, there's nothing else for me to do.

And though my heart went out to him in his boy's
misery, my head said to me, he will recover, but we will
never.

His voice rose into a kind of protest.

— She wanted that door to close on me, Tante. It was as
though she had wiped me out.

He shook his head.

— I can't believe it, he said. I can't believe it.

— It's nothing to do with you, I said.

— I'd have protected her, Tante.

— You couldn't, I said. A *predikant* can't marry a wife that
hides. But apart from that, she wants to go back to father
and mother and childhood, and be safe again.

— She told me she loved me more than all, Tante.

— Ah.

So he went on his sudden holiday, and never returned,
having been called to some other church; and there I trust
that he forgot us. But we were reminded of him, for he was
chosen to play for South Africa, and had his name in all the
papers.

Yes, I understood her, and I understood that she could
let him go without tears, and even wait impatient for the
door to close upon him. The truth is her grief and shame

were greater than her love. The truth is we were not as other people any more.

I thanked God I was in the captain's house, and could put my hands on the walls of my room and feel them solid, and could not hear what was said in the streets and houses. For I could see, when the people passed, that they looked at the captain's house, as they looked at my brother's house, with the front blinds down, and the front door locked, they said, and never to be opened. The schoolchildren walked past it also, not once but many times, talking with lowered voices as they drew near, then falling silent, looking furtively, till that van Belkum, whom I had taken for a fool, angrily forbade them to pass it at all. They walked past the house of the ex-lieutenant too, till that also was forbidden; but he, before he was moved away, knew that they were passing, and by them was made to drink the cup of wrath.

So I sat there in the safety of my room, with the secret book. I should have liked to open it, but that he had said, *if Nella wishes.* What he could not tell to any man, nor any woman, he had written in a book. I took up the big envelope, and could have opened it, had I not been forbidden. And even then I could have opened it. Therefore I put it in a drawer, telling myself I must take it soon.

And as I closed the drawer, there was a knock at the door, and my nephew Frans was there.

— Mother wants you, he said. Father is dead.

XXXIX

So Jakob van Vlaanderen died, eight days after he had been struck down. He died alone, and no one knew he was dead until my sister-in-law found him, bowed over the Book of Job. I remembered the drunken fool, and his asking, what's the point of living, what's the point of life? And my brother's answer in the voice of thunder, the point of living is to serve the Lord your God, and to uphold the honour of your church and language and people. But now he had no answer, and sought hungrily in the Book. Therefore I wrote truly when I said he was destroyed.

My sister-in-law went to Buitenverwagting, to see about the funeral, she said; but she took the secret book. She went in the early morning and did not return till night; but when she came, she brought Nella and the children with her. What they said to one another, and whether they read in the book, I do not know, but the girl came back, silent but steadfast, borne on the strong deep river of this woman's love, that sustained us all.

My brother was buried privately at Buitenverwagting,

with his fathers before him. Had things been otherwise, the whole town and countryside would have been there, and people from Johannesburg and Pretoria, and all the Members of Parliament that he had called in jest his span of oxen.

Then the front door of the house in van Onselen Street was opened, and the blinds rolled up, for my sister-in-law said, something must go out of this house; and she and I no longer hid ourselves, because of her will. But she had already resigned as President of the Women's Welfare Committee, and although they had not yet chosen another, and could have made her President again if they would, yet in the end they chose Elisabet Wagenaar, who is surely one of the world's most stupid women.

And I write down here that we were there when they sentenced him, not only his mother and I, but his wife Nella as well, all of us thinking that to be our duty. Therefore we heard those words, that a man had been unfaithful to his trust, unfit for his position, unworthy of the love of wife and children.

But it is not true what the newspapers said, that he smiled at us when they took him away. For I can see him now with my eyes. And I say that he bowed to us, humbly and gravely, and did not smile at all.

Now what is yet to come I do not know, except that they will go to some other country, far from us all. I trust they will find some peace there, even if he is to be for ever so silent and so grave. And I too, having lived this story in grief and passion, close it in some kind of peace, remembering God's mercy, Who gave us all such friends.

Yet my grief can still come back to me, when I read of some tragic man who has broken the iron law. Was he two men, one brave and gentle, and one tormented? And has he friends, or will he suffer his whole life long? And was there one perhaps, who knew why he had barred the door of his soul and should have hammered on it and cried out not ceasing?

And I grieve for him, and the house he has made to fall with him, not as with Samson the house of his enemies, but the house of his own flesh and blood. And I grieve for the nation which gave him birth, that left the trodden and the known for the vast and secret continent, and made there songs of *heimwee* and longing, and the iron laws. And now the Lord has turned our captivity, I pray we shall not walk arrogant, remembering Herod whom an Angel of the Lord struck down, for that he made himself a god.

But most I grieve for Frans and his wife who live now solitary at Buitenverwagting. The boy Koos is tall and dark, and seems to have some special mark on him of solitariness. Will they say when they meet him, *where have I heard your name?* And will that trouble him, or is he troubled already? Ah, I pray the world will let it be forgotten.

Now all that I have written here is true, for I have seen the secret book, and all the things he wrote in prison; and my sister-in-law says it is true, though parts she would have written otherwise. And I wish she could have written it, for maybe of the power of her love that never sought itself, men would have turned to the holy task of pardon, that the body of the Lord might not be wounded twice, and virtue come of our offences.

Glossary

Afrikaner	A descendant of the original Dutch settlers, who came to South Africa three hundred years ago
Afrikaans	A supple and simplified version of the original Dutch language brought to South Africa
Ag	An exclamation with guttural "g", not quite translatable, but close to similar expressions in Scottish and Irish dialect
Baas	Master
Boerewors	Form of sausage made on South African farms
Boomslang	Tree snake
Diaken	A lay official of the Dutch Reformed Church
Dorp	Village
Frikkadel	Mincemeat
Goeie middag	Good afternoon
Goeie môre	Good morning
Goeie nag	Good night
Heimwee	Nostalgic longing for home or homeland. Compare Scottish "hamewith"
Hemel	An exclamation similar to the English "Good Heavens"
Ja	Yes
Khaki bos	The khaki weed that has a pungent smell
Kleinbasie	Little master
Klonkies	Small black boys
Kloof	Ravine
Koeksusters	An Afrikaner delicacy
Konfyt	A preserve
Liedjies	Songs
Liefste	Dearest

Magtig	An exclamation like the English "Good gracious"
Melktert	An Afrikaner delicacy
Meneer	Sir
Morgen	Measure of land, just over two acres
Nee	No
Oubaas	Old master
Pan	A sheet of water, very often circular in shape, found frequently in parts of the grass country
Pannekoek	An Afrikaner delicacy
Phalarope	A small migrant wading bird, occasionally straying from the coasts to inland waters
Pietmevrou	The South African whippoorwill. Both these names are onomatopoeic
Predikant	Minister of the Dutch Reformed Church
Ruitertjie	Another small wading bird
Sitkamer	Drawing-room
Volkswelsyn-beampte	Social Welfare officer